The Sticky Buns Challenge

Sticky Notes Series

Book Two or standalone

Sherri Schoenborn Murray

Visit Sherri's website:
www.christianromances.com

The Sticky Buns Challenge
Christian Romances LLC

Story edit by Patty Slack.
Contributing editors: Cori Murray, Ethel Schoenborn, and
Pamela Waddell, and final editor Kristi Weber.
Photo credit: Alison Meyer Photography
Printed in the U.S.A.

To my son—
Casey Murray
Thank you for being my taste tester
and for your
blatantly honest remarks.
And,
to Elaine Peterson,
for letting me write down
all the funny things you say.
And, for being such a dear friend
to my mom, Ethel.

*For the entire law is fulfilled
in keeping this one command:
"Love your neighbor as yourself."*
Galatians 5:14 NIV

Chapter One

September 5, 2002 – Moscow, Idaho

Late afternoon, Ethel King pulled together a spur-of-the-moment Scrabble party at her home with her good friends—Mildred, Betty, and Sharon. Wouldn't you know it, she got stuck with Sharon. Out of all the years they'd been playing Scrabble, the best word Sharon had ever played was onyx. For Sharon to come up with a word like onyx was proof that she and Mildred had cheated. That was the night when Sharon kept making trips to the bathroom, probably with a mini-dictionary tucked inside her knee-high.

Mildred carefully swiveled the board to face Sharon for her turn. The best options ever available in a game of Scrabble lay before her. There were three open vowels, several easy consonants, and what does she spell…?

Cuba. Ethel read the word upside down.

"You can't use proper names, Sharon." Even though they were partners, Ethel called her on it.

"It's not just the name of a country." Sharon wore a lightweight cardigan over the top of her royal blue polyester dress with large hibiscus flowers. Her pearl cluster earrings were probably clip-ons.

"What else is it, Sharon?" Betty sounded patient enough.

"It's a Cuba this and a cube of that."

"A cube of this, not a Cuba this," Ethel tried to keep her voice level. "They're two completely different words." Why did Sharon even play? She was the world's worst speller. They were going to be fifty points behind before it was even Ethel's turn.

Sharon took the "a" off Cuba, earning them a whopping seven points.

"As I was saying—" Tiles in hand, Betty studied the board. "I always buy unsalted butter, and when my daughter visits, she hates to make toast. She salts her toast when she's at my place. She says there's no flavor if she doesn't."

"Does she pepper it, too?" Sharon asked.

"Huh?'

The shrill of the phone ringing halted their conversation. Everyone who usually called Ethel was seated at her maple dinette set in the living room. Though, the caller might also be Quinn, Katherine, or her neighbor Joyce Wooten.

Ethel strode to the curio cabinet and lifted the receiver to her ear. "Hello."

"Hi, Ethel, it's Sandy."

"Eleven points," Betty said, turning the board.

"Hi, Sandy. Hold on a second. The girls are here, and it's my turn." Stretching the phone cord, Ethel returned to the table. The F she'd been eyeing earlier was still open, so she spelled toff. Her first F landed on a triple-letter score. "Eighteen points," she told Mildred, the scorekeeper.

"Is that a word?" Sharon asked.

"Wanna challenge your own partner?" Mildred glanced back and forth between the two.

Ethel covered the receiver. "It is. I've played it before."

"Whatever you say." Sharon waved a hand.

Mildred gave them both a few more seconds before tallying their points.

"Hi, Sandy." Ethel returned to the phone and with her back to the girls, was able to finally give attention to her only daughter-in-law who didn't call her Mom.

"Hi. It sounds like you're busy, so I'll get right to the point. Michael wanted me to call you and discuss the possibility of Jimmy living with you this fall."

"This fall?" The University of Idaho's fall semester had started more than two weeks ago. Ethel's stomach dropped. "I thought Jimmy was living in the dorms." He'd stopped by once when she'd been grocery shopping and left a note on her back door.

The girls hushed behind her.

"He didn't qualify for as much financial aid as we'd hoped. It's all been a mess."

"Where is he living?"

"At home."

"Home?" Lewiston was at least a forty-five-minute commute one way, and with the pass, would be a terrible drive in the winter.

"He's been working at Bill's Tires here in town, and his boss just informed him today that they approved his transfer to the Moscow store. With Katherine living in Potlatch for the semester, we thought there might be a chance . . ." Sandy's voice trailed off.

"Well, it's very sudden."

"I know it is, and I don't want to keep you. I know you have company."

Ethel stared at her green shag carpeting, and with a knot in her belly remembered Tim, the last grandson who'd lived with her while attending the U of I.

"After Tim, I promised myself I would never have another boy."

"Well, we all know that Jimmy's nothing like Tim," Sandy said.

Tim, Ethel's oldest grandson, had been a Casanova on steroids.

"He's a good kid, Ethel. He could help around the place—mow the lawn, fix things, weatherize, change the oil. He knows how to do all that."

"I'm going to have to pray about it." Next week she'd be perfecting her cinnamon rolls for the fair, and now, if she said yes to Jimmy, she could very well be moving in another grandchild.

"I understand. Let us know what you decide."

"I will, honey." Ethel hung up the receiver and returned to the table for her turn. "Sorry, girls." She shook her head.

"What's going on, Ethel?" Sharon wiggled her hand into the little cloth bag for letters.

"That was Sandy, Michael's wife. They're wondering if Jimmy can move in with me. He didn't get enough financial aid."

"What's Jimmy like?" Sharon asked.

"He has his AA from Lewiston Community College in something, and now he wants to get his BA in . . ." Ethel's gaze roved the ceiling to no avail. "He's a sweetheart and cute."

"A cute sweetheart." Sharon smiled.

"Is he another ladies' man?" Betty asked.

"No, thank heaven. He's not like Tim."

"I think you should write a pros-and-cons list." Mildred's voice was raspy like she might still be smoking, even though she claimed she wasn't. "It's not like you're having him over for just the weekend. Your other grandkids have stayed years."

When Katherine had moved to Potlatch for a temporary teaching position two weeks ago, Ethel had tried to look at the bright side of living alone: less laundry, fewer groceries to buy, easier meal planning. She'd forgotten how quiet it could be in the evenings alone by herself with the cuckoo clock. Several times already, she'd resorted to having pears and cottage cheese for dinner.

"What's he like? What's his personality?" Sharon asked.

"He's not as determined, stubborn, or brilliant as Katherine. He's a little more sensitive. He was the toddler who'd cry if you took a toy away, while Katherine, she'd just grab it right back."

"Jimmy and Ethel," Sharon said like they were already living together.

"Sometimes it's easy to feel used, isn't it?" Mildred eyed the board for her turn.

What had Pastor Ken said? We can make a difference for Christ in someone's life, but all too often we don't because our big old fat self gets in the way. Jimmy needed her. Her grandson needed her. How could she possibly say no?

"Used is the wrong word." Ethel rose from the table and dialed Sandy's number.

"Hello, Kings' residence," Jimmy answered, his voice smooth and masculine.

"Jimmy, your mom called here about ten minutes ago. I must have been tired to even have to think about you living here. You can stay in Katherine's old room, and as long as you help me with things that need to be done, don't have friends stay past eleven o'clock, or play your music too loud, or . . ." She started thinking about all the things Tim had put her through. "Well, honey, you're not Tim. When do you want to move in?"

"My last day of work here is uh . . . Tuesday. How's next Wednesday, Grandma?"

"Fine . . ." Her cinnamon rolls were supposed to be delivered to the fair Wednesday afternoon, but it was fine.

Everything would work out. It always did. She hung up and returned to the table.

"That didn't take you too long to decide." Sharon reached into the letter bag.

"One grandchild to the next like a factory." Mildred shook her head.

"The King factory," Ethel said, glancing at the board. Sharon's last word was: T-I-N. In one word, she'd wasted three of the easiest to use letters in the English language.

"How many points did you get?" Mildred waited, pencil in hand.

"Three," Sharon said.

Maybe Jimmy would play Scrabble. Ethel peered around the table at the girls. After Jimmy moved in, he could be her partner, and they wouldn't even need to invite Sharon. Before she could stop herself, she clapped her hands together, thrilled.

"What is it?" Sharon locked eyes with her.

"Nothing!" Ethel wiggled in her chair and, biting her lower lip, realized the error of her ways. Not a soul in the world had a sweeter disposition than Sharon. Too bad she was terrible at Scrabble.

"It had to be something. Something to do with Jimmy," Betty pried in her Amarillo accent. Betty and her late husband had been stationed at the Air Force base there for thirty years, and even though she'd now lived in Idaho for over a decade, her tongue had never left Texas.

"He . . ." Ethel tried to think up something honest. "He plays guitar. He's pretty good. Katherine liked to bake, but Jimmy plays guitar. I forgot that about him."

"Well, it's odd that you squealed about something you forgot," Mildred said.

"I suppose it is," Ethel said, eyeing the word T-I-N.

Chapter Two

On Wednesday morning, a car that reminded Ethel of the *Dukes of Hazzard* television show rolled into her gravel parking area out back. Her grandson couldn't have arrived at a better time. Her Rhodes dough was in the fridge, thawing. She went out the back door and started down the narrow concrete walkway.

His two-door car was a shimmery, mint-green mouthwash color. The tires in the back were taller than the ones in the front, reminding her that her grandson had been working in a tire shop for the last couple of years while he put himself through community college. He swung the driver's side door closed behind him and rounded the rear of the vehicle.

He was taller than she'd remembered. His shoulders were wider, too. Even though he had a dark beard and mustache, many a girl was going to find him a heartthrob. Nope, their Jimmy wasn't a scrawny teenager anymore.

He looked like a man.

What had she gotten herself into?

"Hi, Grandma." He gave her a full-on hug. "Sorry, it's been so long." He stepped back to admire her.

She gulped, looking up at him. "You missed Christmas. You had the flu."

"I missed Easter, too, for some reason." His warm brown eyes had covetously long lashes, curly since the day he was born. He wasn't a spindly thing anymore. He was as solid as the bronze statue of Teddy Roosevelt on the U of I campus.

"You look shipshape," she managed. Was it too late to change her mind? Maybe she should pull money out of Edwin's pension to pay for Jimmy to have a room in the dorms.

"It's from working at the tire shop, Grandma."

Returning to his car, he opened the trunk. It was stuffed to the brim. "Do you have a DVD player or VHS?" He glanced over at her.

"VHS."

"Mom was right." He grinned.

Ethel had finally updated from her Beta machine. She wasn't about to buy another heavy appliance. She grabbed a pillow and a blanket from the trunk and held the picket gate open for him. He stepped past her, carrying a large box topped with movies.

"Is this your first time living away from home?" Hopefully, it wasn't. He was twenty-two. She hurried up the back steps ahead of him to hold open the door.

"Yes. Mom got a little teary eyed. Dad was fine." Jimmy glanced back at her on his way through the kitchen. "I've missed the smell of your house."

"Oh, what does it smell like?" It couldn't smell like the yeast dough, as the Rhodes was still in the fridge.

"I don't know." One step inside the living room, he paused beside the curio cabinet, smiled and took in the wide ocean painting above the green Naugahyde couch. From there, his gaze panned right to the white brick fireplace, the white-painted front door, long lace curtains, the green shag carpeting, and the heavy, old TV in the corner.

"I love how it's always the same. Mom's always redecorating. It's nice returning to a place that's always the same."

"What's it smell like?" She wasn't going to let him be like Katherine—changing the subject whenever she was onto something important.

"The way it always has. It smells like Grandpa and Grandma King's house." He smiled at her softly. Beneath all his manliness, he was still her dear sweet Jimmy.

"If you had to describe the smell of our house, how would you describe it?"

Two steps past the curio cabinet, he transferred the box to one arm and opened the stairwell door. "Well . . ." He glanced back at her. "There's a hint of Grandpa's tobacco."

Tobacco? Edwin had been gone for over ten years. How could the house still smell like his horrible cigars?

"And I think"—Jimmy sniffed the air— "baby powder."

After she toweled off, Ethel always sprinkled baby powder on her feet.

"Don't ever change it." He marched up the steep stairwell to his attic room.

How could he say that? No woman in her right mind wanted her home to smell like cigar smoke.

She thought of her most recent gathering. Of her friends, who would be the most honest? Without question, it was Mildred. While Jimmy was upstairs, Ethel dialed her number and inhaled deeply.

Mildred's raspy voice came on the line.

"Mildred, it's Ethel. Does my house smell like tobacco to you?"

"Good morning, Ethel. Let me think." Mildred took a sip of something, probably coffee. She couldn't think in the morning until she'd had a full cup. "Yes. For the last forty years, your house has smelled like Edwin's cigars. Even here lately, there's been a few times that I've been in your home that the smell has been so distinct I could swear Edwin was sitting in that old recliner of his, puffing away."

Ethel felt her shoulders sink. "Do you smell baby powder, too?"

"If I have, it's very, very faint."

"Thank you, Mildred. I knew I could count on you to be honest. I've always appreciated your honesty."

"It's nice that someone does."

After she hung up, Ethel strode through her small boxy kitchen and opened her Frigidaire for a bottle of Gatorade. She shut the fridge and paused. Where was her Rhodes dough?

She reopened the fridge. It wasn't there. Where was it? She opened the top freezer door and stared at the bag of store-bought dough. Oh, pooh! She hadn't taken it out. Last night after she'd read the directions on the back of the package, she must have simply put it back in the freezer. Of all days to lose her brain!

She'd forgotten to take the dough out of the freezer for one of the most important days of the year. Today, she'd enter her cinnamon rolls in at the fair. Next thing you know, she'd be using a knife in the toaster, going to Tidyman's in her robe and slippers, or forgetting that church was on the east side of town. Maybe Jimmy was a godsend.

How could she forget the dough? Maybe she'd had too much on her noggin with Jimmy moving in. Ethel sighed. *Dear Lord, help me today. I want to earn at least a green ribbon. Brown is dreary. Green is cheery. Amen.*

Ethel took two rock-hard loaves of dough out of the plastic bag and read the instructions for thawing. In two and a half hours, her cinnamon rolls were due at the fairgrounds. Even though *defrost* was not an option on the bag, she set the loaves on a plate and popped them into the microwave. She pressed Defrost, timing it for two pounds.

"Dear Lord, let them be wonderful."

The phone rang. Ethel strolled to the curio cabinet in the living room and picked it up.

"Hello."

"Ethel, it's Joyce. How are you faring?"

"Good," Ethel lied. Joyce, her neighbor from across the street, was also entering the baked goods category.

"Is your dough rising?"

"Yes." Ethel inhaled. It wasn't a lie.

"Good girl. What time did you get up?" Joyce's voice was even more gravelly than normal.

"Seven, the usual time."

"I always get up early for my fair baking days. Sometimes things happen, and I like to give myself ample time in case I need it. As we speak, my dinner rolls are shaped and having a second rise."

"My dough is already in the oven." Heat gathered in Ethel's cheeks. It wasn't a lie—the microwave was often referred to as an oven.

"Well, you're ahead of me for once. I spent a great deal of the morning trying to find my dinner roll recipe. I'd misfiled it under quick breads instead of yeast breads. I don't know what I was thinking. Thank goodness we have until eight o'clock tonight."

"Eight o'clock. I thought the deadline was one."

"No, the entry period is from three to eight o'clock. What time did you say you got up this morning?" Joyce asked.

"Seven."

"Did you refrigerate your dough overnight?"

"No, I forgot to take it out of the freezer."

"How in the world are they already in the oven?"

"Well, the package says to thaw them in the fridge, but my dough is presently in the *microwave* oven."

"What do you mean *the package*?"

"The Rhodes dough package."

"Ethel! You can't use store-bought dough. Didn't you read the rules? Everything has to be from scratch. No packaged mixes of any type."

There went her green ribbon.

Ethel stretched the phone cord behind her and paused near the window where she had a view of Joyce's little white house across Logan Street.

"If you start now, you'll still have time to get them in," Joyce said.

"Do you have a dough recipe I can borrow?" Ethel bit the insides of her cheeks. For years, she'd been after Joyce's recipe.

"You know, I don't share my recipes. Now, you need to get off the phone and read the rules."

Ethel heaved a sigh. She'd had such high hopes for today.

In the kitchen, she thumbed through the *Breads* file in her wooden recipe box. Years ago, Patty, her daughter-in-law, had tole painted *Ethel's Succulents* on the front of the box. She wished she'd painted *Ethel's Edibles.* Succulents were a cactus.

From amidst the piles of papers on the table in the kitchen, she found the rule booklet for the fair. She had to unearth her magnifying glass because the text was so tiny. Pushing her glasses higher up the bridge of her nose, she hovered the thick lens over the fine print of the Latah County Fair Baked Goods section. *All entries in Baked Food and Confection Classes must be home prepared by the exhibitor. Entries must be from scratch and must not contain packaged mixes.*

Oh, pooh. For the last month, she'd been planning to use her cheater cinnamon roll recipe. It was so easy and delicious. Thawing the dough was the toughest part. Hmm . . . If she cheated, how would they ever know? Desperate times called for desperate measures. She continued reading. *Recipe card must accompany entry.*

"Oh, pooh." Ethel's shoulders sank.

The rules in the cinnamon roll section read: *Bring four rolls on a paper plate or in a Ziploc bag.* The last line of the Baked Goods section was: *Entries will be judged for appearance, texture, and taste. Good luck, Queenies.*

She was seventy-one years old, had never placed higher than eighth at the fair, and now they were going to disadvantage her even more and not let her use her cheater dough.

It wasn't fair.

Jimmy carried his last box upstairs and surveyed the attic room. It was plenty big enough. There was the full-sized bed, a large oval-shaped mirror above a squatty dresser and, taking up half of the room, a red and gray block quilt stretched on a rack. Since his childhood, it had awaited Grandma's finishing touches.

He glanced at the round-faced clock on the nightstand. In twenty minutes, he needed to be at Bill's Tires to meet his new boss. He felt blessed for the transfer. With school, car insurance, and gas, the Lord knew he needed the money.

After setting the box of videos on top of the dresser, he started down the steep, shag-carpeted stairs. The stairwell door creaked closed behind him.

"Perfect timing," Grandma said from the kitchen. "Wash your hands, Jimmy. I'll have you knead the dough. It hurts my wrists."

He washed up at the sink and hoped kneading wouldn't take too long

"I get so frustrated with this part of *scratch*"—with floured fingers, Grandma did air quotes—"that I just want to throw the dough against the wall. I'm so glad you're here." She smiled.

"Wh . . . what do I do?"

"Well, you push your palm down heavy into the dough." She curled her fingers, jutting forth her palm. "And then you knead it. Think of wrestling like you'd see on TV. It's a lot like that, except you always keep the dough in the flour." She sprinkled flour on the cutting board.

He wrestled the dough around the wooden board a dozen times and glanced over his shoulder to where she stood in front of the stove.

"I'll set the timer, honey. You'll need to do this for ten minutes."

"Ten minutes!" He chuckled. "That's all I can, Grandma. I'm meeting my new boss at Bill's Tires at one o'clock. I start work tomorrow."

"How many hours a week do you plan to work?" Behind her glasses, her twinkly eyes studied him.

"Twenty hours a week. I have to, for gas and insurance."

"You should just walk."

"No, way."

"That's what Katherine did. She walked everywhere."

"Not me. That car's my baby. My life." He shook his head. There's no way he'd leave it back in Lewiston or parked in Grandma's driveway, for that matter.

Jimmy's new commute to work was less than half of a mile. Situated on the cusp of downtown, Bill's Tires had a great corner location. Right in front of the store, Highway 95 slowed to a residential pace.

Bill's Tires, a family-owned company, had six northern Idaho and Southwest Washington locations. Three years ago, Mike Gregerson, the manager of the Lewiston branch had taken a chance on him—a punk kid with no prior work experience. He'd worked hard to prove himself.

Following employee policy, Jimmy parked in the back lot. Then, he strode around the side of the bright white building with royal blue signage and entered through the glass double doors.

A middle-aged man with gray, slicked-back hair stood behind the showroom counter.

"I'm here to see Vance."

"That's me. You must be James King." Vance glanced at the clock. "You're on time—exactly on time. In the future… get here five minutes before your shift starts. Never right on time." He talked slow, then fast, like his thoughts came in bursts. "You already have a uniform?"

"Yes, and I go by Jimmy."

"Three pairs of dark blue pants . . . and three shirts?"

"Yes."

"I never want to see wrinkles in your uniform. You're to wear your hair like mine. And the men who work for me… have to use Brylcreem."

Brylcreem? Jimmy blinked.

Vance looked like Fonzie from *Happy Days,* except he was older and taller, at least five ten, as he was only a few inches shorter than Jimmy.

"You pat it here and here, and run your hand down the middle," Vance ran a hand through the side of his hair, "and you'll have hair like mine."

Over his shoulder, Jimmy scanned the floor for other employees. Was it really a requirement? Did the other guys wear their hair like this? At Jimmy's old job in Lewiston, no one wore Brylcreem. But . . . Vance hadn't been his boss.

"You need to be clean shaven. No facial hair for any of my employees. A lot of our customers are offended by facial hair, especially the older generation."

Santa had a beard. No one seemed to mind that. But Jimmy didn't say it out loud.

"I want you here at seven thirty sharp. We open at eight."

"Seven thirty sharp." Jimmy nodded.

"You weren't listening. What'd I tell you?"

His stomach dropped. "Five minutes early. So, you want me here at seven twenty-five?"

"Yeah. You got it." Vance's eyes didn't waver or glimmer. The guy was dead serious. "The only place in town that carries Brylcreem is the drug store on Third and Main."

"Third and Main," Jimmy said, trying to remember. His new boss was proof that he wasn't in Lewiston anymore.

Chapter Three

All baked goods were due at the fair by eight p.m. With a nervous twist in her belly, Ethel studied Katherine's cinnamon roll recipe that she'd used for the dough. Then she studied her Cheater Cinnamon Rolls recipe. Only a few months ago, she'd clipped this easy new favorite from the newspaper. Although she couldn't use Rhodes dough, she could still follow the rest of the instructions.

Powdered sugar, cinnamon, butter; one by one, she set the ingredients on the counter. She noticed the carton of whipping cream was already opened. She remembered buying it, but she didn't remember opening it. She briefly sniffed it. Katherine must have opened it last week for Quinn when they'd visited. He liked cream in his coffee.

Using a small whisk, she combined the powdered sugar and cream and divided the thin glaze between two glass pans. Then she peered at the newspaper recipe. *Pour the mixture into two greased 9 x 9 pans.* "Yes, I did that." She glanced back at her recipe. Except she'd forgotten to *grease* the pan!

She was doing just terrible.

"Please, Lord, don't let me be the only baker to mess up today." She poured the icing mixture back into the bowl, washed the pans, and tried to calm her nerves. "And help me to have a brain. These rolls are important."

Once she'd given her ineptness to the Lord, the rest of the cinnamon roll preparation went smoothly. She brushed the rolled dough with melted butter, spread the mixture of cinnamon and brown sugar over the top, and even found herself humming.

She thought of her neighbor, Joyce, who was the epitome of the perfect baker. For the last five years in-a-row, she'd earned a third-place ribbon for her dinner rolls. It was nice that they were in different categories; that way, they could root each other on and not feel too competitive.

While the rolls had their second rise, Ethel cleaned up the mess she'd made and then relaxed for a spell in her recliner with a crossword puzzle. Before she knew it, the timer dinged. She returned to the kitchen and lifted the damp tea towel covering the rolls. They'd risen beautifully.

She set the oven for 350-degrees and made a pot of coffee. When the oven was ready, she slid the pans inside and spun the egg timer to twenty-two minutes.

The next step was to write out the recipe card that would accompany her rolls to the fair. She sat down at the table and, readying her pen, glanced back and forth from her newspaper recipe to Katherine's handwritten recipe.

Where had her mind been? Instead of one teaspoon of cinnamon like her cheater roll recipe called for, she'd put in the full tablespoon called for in Katherine's recipe. And while her recipe only called for a half cup of brown sugar, hadn't she used three-quarters of a cup? And her recipe didn't call for nutmeg, but she'd still added a pinch.

Ethel held the magnifier over the recipe card and peered at her granddaughter's tiny print. One-third cup sugar. She could have sworn that she added a half cup to the dough. Maybe she needed new bifocals. To write down exactly what she'd done was a complete guessing game. She clamped a hand to her forehead and sighed.

"Oh, Lord, please let my mistakes be providentially delicious."

She needed big-time prayer. She made her way to the phone and dialed her neighbor's number. On several occasions, Joyce had prayed with her. "Joyce . . ."

"Ethel, how are your cinnamon rolls faring?"

"I need prayer. I accidentally combined two recipes into one, and it's too late to do anything about it because they're already in the oven."

"Well, I made my leftover dinner roll dough into cinnamon rolls, and Mike Morrison—you know Mike, the president of the U of I?"

"Yes, of course. Only this summer, I—"

"Well, his wife Virginia and I are good friends. Virginia stopped by unexpectedly. She's not much of a baker, so I had her sample one of my cinnamon rolls, and she convinced me that I need to enter them into the fair."

"Oh, I see. Does this mean you won't be praying for mine?"

"If I did pray for your rolls, Ethel, I'd pray that they take second place to mine. Do you really want me to pray that?"

Being second to Joyce would be better than her usual brown-place finish. "If your rolls are as wonderful as Virginia says, I don't mind taking second place to you."

"In that case, I'll pray."

Eyes closed, Ethel listened to Joyce's prayer and mumbled a few thoughts of her own. While they were on the phone, she heard the back door click open and closed. Jimmy was home. He gently patted her shoulder as he stepped past her, and then headed straight to the bathroom, holding a small brown sack.

Her heart warmed. The Lord had blessed her in her old age to have the company of such a sweet grandson.

"Did I tell you that Jimmy moved in today? He's such a wonderful young man, except he just carried a brown paper bag into the bathroom."

"Oh no . . . flashback," Joyce said. "Remember your other grandson and his little episodes in your bathroom. What's in the bag?"

"I don't know. I've been on the phone with you."

"What size was it?"

"Uh . . . the size of a lunch bag with an apple and a small thermos in it."

"It doesn't sound good. I asked Bridget, my great-niece, to live with me, you know. She said maybe next year. She wants to make friends in the dorms her first year. She's been told that once you're off campus, it's very difficult to make friends. I think she's right, Ethel. Look at Katherine. She didn't have any friends, and her boyfriend ended up being a professor."

The bathroom door creaked open. "Grandma, do you have scissors?"

"I gotta go, Joyce. Jimmy needs scissors."

"What does he need scissors for? Be careful."

"I will. What kind of scissors, honey?" Ethel hung up the phone and walked toward the hallway.

"Hair scissors would be great." The bathroom door clicked closed.

Hopefully, he was trimming his beard. She'd never been fond of beards. In the hallway closet, the hair-cutting kit sat next to the shoe polishing box. She held the scissors in one hand and knocked on the white painted door with her other.

He opened it a foot wide for the hand off. "Thanks, Grandma, you're the best."

No hint of cigarette smoke filtered out, or that skunky smoke smell that Tim used to say was incense.

"No, honey, *you're* the best." Why Tim had burned incense in the bathroom was beyond her. She needed to stop comparing her two grandsons. They were related, but thank heaven, that's where the similarities ended.

The last thing Ethel wanted to do was make a mess in the kitchen again. So, after she delivered her cinnamon rolls to the 4-H Building at the Latah County Fairgrounds, she stopped at Safeway to purchase something easy for supper. She opted for a layered bean dip and a bag of tortilla chips. Cleanup didn't get much simpler than that.

That evening they had several things to celebrate: Ethel entering her rolls in the fair; Jimmy's new look—he was so handsome without his beard and mustache, and their first night batching together. After sharing the wonderful bean dip, Ethel made a pot of decaf coffee to go along with dessert— her made-from-scratch cinnamon rolls.

"Grandma, do you have half-and-half?" Jimmy searched the fridge.

"No, but there's whipping cream, which is even richer."

He set the carton on the table, plus the can of Reddi-Wip topping. Ethel had forgotten that he liked to pipe whipped cream on top of his coffee and made a mental sticky note to stock up on it the next time she went grocery shopping.

"This looks good." Jimmy surveyed the three-inch-high, golden cinnamon roll on his plate.

"I told you about how I'd combined the two recipes. Now, for the moment of truth." Ethel watched as he took his first bite.

Closing his eyes, he savored the experience. He swished his mouth around, looking at her.

"It's delicious. I mean, this is really good."

"You think so?" He looked like he meant it.

He nodded. "It's delicious."

Ethel stirred a teaspoon of sugar into her coffee. After the morning she'd had, it was amazing to think she might win a ribbon. Maybe even a green ribbon. Her past entries had taught her to not set her sights too high.

Jimmy turned the carton of whipping cream toward her. "Do you know this is past date? September fifth." He pointed to the label.

"I sniffed it earlier. It's fine." Besides, today was only the twelfth.

Jimmy held the carton beneath his nose and took a big old whiff. Grimacing, he careened back in the chair. "Whoa, it's sour!" Off to his left, he held the carton as far away as possible.

"Here, let me see." She'd sniffed it only a few hours ago. It couldn't have gone that sour in so short a time. She took a deeper whiff than she'd taken earlier in the day and in a state of olfactory agony nearly fell out of her chair.

Her rolls! Oh no, her beautiful rolls! Ethel's hands flew to her face. On the first day of the fair, the baked goods already had ribbons, which meant that the judges taste-tested everything either tonight or before the start of the fair at one o'clock tomorrow. Of all days for her cream to go bad.

"Grandma, it's no big deal. I can use this." Jimmy shook the can of Reddi-Wip and, starting with the outer edge of his cup, swirled around until the dark coffee was frothy white on top. "Everything's better with whipped cream, Grandma."

Feeling sick to her stomach, Ethel rose from her chair and poured the remaining lumpy cream down the sink. Even after she'd thoroughly rinsed the carton, it smelled too sour to leave in the house. Arm extended away from her, she started for the back door.

"Grandma, these rolls are amazing. They have an awesome aftertaste. Like sourdough."

She halted beside Jimmy's chair, staring at him. "What'd you say?"

"I said 'there's a nice aftertaste, like sourdough.' Here, I'll throw that away for you." He took the carton from her.

While he retreated out the back door, Ethel lowered herself to her chair and stared at his empty plate. She'd used the whipping cream in the glaze in the bottom of the pan, placed the rolls on top, and baked them. Was Jimmy going to be sick for his first day at his new job? Was she going to get all the Baked Goods judges sick at the fair? Her cinnamon rolls looked so innocent. Were they weapons of mass destruction?

Jimmy returned and washed his hands at the sink, humming.

She had to tell him.

He sat down and immediately reached for another roll.

"Jim-meee!"

Leaning back in the chair, he stared wide-eyed at her.

"Is it all right if I have another one, Grandma? Or do you have plans for them?"

"I mixed half a cup of *that* whipping cream," she gulped, pointed to the back door, "with powdered sugar for a glaze for the bottom of the pan. My cinnamon rolls baked in it."

His brows gathered. "It's just soured milk. That's what cheese is—soured milk. I wouldn't worry."

Famous last words. Or was there a scientific possibility that soured cream lost its rancidness when baked?

"Can I have one more?" He inched his hand toward the glass pie plate.

"Shoot yourself."

She sipped her cup of decaf and watched him devour another roll. If he, not to mention all the judges, were going to get sick, she supposed she might as well, too.

It was only fair.

She set a golden-brown roll on her plate. Using her fork, she tore off a small chunk and took her first bite. The tablespoon of cinnamon had been a delicious mistake, and the dough had a nice, soft chew. She smacked her lips together. Like Jimmy had claimed—there was a pleasant sourdough aftertaste.

Surprisingly pleasant. She giggled.

They were delicious.

Jimmy poured himself a second cup of coffee and crowned it with another round of whipped topping.

"I hope you don't put that on your breakfast cereal," Ethel said.

He eyed her stash of boxes to the right of the sink, where she kept them stored on the counter. Same as always—Fiber One and Total. Katherine had finished off the last of the Smart Start.

He grinned. "Maybe I will."

After dinner, Ethel worked on a crossword puzzle in the comfy corduroy recliner while Jimmy watched TV. In the last half hour, her stomach had knotted up enough that she worried she might be getting sick. Hopefully, it was only because of the bean dip.

During the commercial break, Jimmy gathered up their water glasses, put them in the dishwasher, and then she heard the thud of the back door. He returned a short while later, not missing any of his show.

"Is everything okay?" she asked.

"Yep." He flopped down on the length of the couch, crossing his hands behind his head.

The next set of commercials, he went out the back door again. This time, he was outside for a whole car commercial before he returned to plop back down on the couch.

"Is your stomach upset?" Might as well not beat around the bush. They were going to be living together for the next couple of years.

"Just a little." He glanced over at her. "It's only the beans, Grandma."

His attempt at reassurance confirmed that he thought her cinnamon rolls might very well be the culprit.

Dear Lord . . . Ethel closed her eyes and launched a missile-sized prayer. *Please let it be the beans. I don't want to get all the judges sick at the fair. I finally made something delicious.*

"If we get sick, Jimmy, you know what it means? I'll have to go to the fair tomorrow and withdraw my rolls."

"I hope that doesn't happen, Grandma."

"Me, too."

Jimmy's flatulence during commercials continued. What a gentleman he was, letting himself outside every time. She giggled as he plopped himself down on the Naugahyde couch for about the tenth time that evening.

"Still think it's the beans?"

"Yep." He grinned at her. "Without a doubt."

"Goodnight, Edwin." Ethel touched a kissed finger to her late husband's picture on the nightstand before turning out the light. A sliver of light from the tall streetlamp filtered through the edge of the blinds and across her chenille bedspread near her toes. "Jimmy's a man now," she whispered. "He was always your favorite because he was still hugging you, even when he was twelve. Remember that?

"I made the most delicious cinnamon rolls today. You wouldn't have believed it, except there may be possible side effects."

Her heart knotted. "Dear Lord, let it be the beans."

Ethel lay awake waiting for Montezuma's revenge to strike. She listened for footsteps overhead, for the stairwell door to fling open, and for Jimmy to streak to the bathroom. And, in the silence of waiting, she fell asleep.

Chapter Four

Jimmy wouldn't tell Grandma, but her cinnamon rolls could easily be nicknamed *Cinnamon Blasts.* While he crunched through a bowl of Fiber One, Grandma popped two cinnamon rolls into the microwave.

"Don't worry, Jimmy, I heated one up for you. I know how much you enjoyed them last night."

She was testing him. If he refused, she was going to withdraw them from the fair.

While Grandma slathered butter on top of the warm rolls, he squirted a round of whipped cream on top of his coffee. At least she was having another one, too.

The warm cinnamon roll was again delicious. He flashed her a smile of encouragement.

"You look so handsome in your uniform. Does Bill's Tires have a laundry service?"

"No, Les Schwab does because their guys get really greasy. They do mechanical work. We're just tires."

"Just tires." Grandma narrowed her eyes like she was trying to picture it.

"Don't let me forget, I need to Brylcreem my hair before I leave."

"Brylcreem? I haven't heard of anyone using Brylcreem for years."

"This manager requires everyone to wear their hair like his."

"Elvis style?" Eyes closed, Grandma savored her first bite of roll.

"Sorta." Jimmy shrugged. "I'd say more like Fonzie-style."

"Sounds like Bill's Tires is old-fashioned. I like that." Grandma patted the table between them. "I want to take a picture of you before you leave. You look so handsome without that beard."

And probably younger. That's what everyone usually told him when he didn't wear a beard. He sighed, stroking his bare cheek.

A few minutes later, Jimmy Brylcreemed his bangs in the bathroom mirror. They curled over into an old-fashioned wave. He rubbed a quarter teaspoon of the goop between his hands and ran them through the sides of his hair for the Fonzie look. He glanced at his profile. What would Allison, his ex-girlfriend, think of his hair?

Knowing her, she'd come up with a goofy saying and print it on a T-shirt.

Grandma had him stand in front of the white picket gate with his car in the background while she held up her old Polaroid camera.

"Do they still make film for that?"

"Of course. Now, smile." Her elbows went horizontal for the shot.

He grinned, recalling one of the loud blasts he'd made in the backyard last night.

"Have a wonderful day at work, honey." She angled the picture toward her, away from the sunlight.

"Thank you." Hopefully, she wasn't going to take pictures of him every morning before he left for work. While she stood near the back gate, fluttering kissed fingers, he backed his '75 Mercury Cougar out of the gravel driveway.

A block later, he turned right onto the Troy Highway. After less than a half mile, he parked behind Bill's Tires. Then he rounded the side of the building and strode through the first open bay on his way to the showroom. The air compressors were already on and building up pressure. In the reception area, a stocky weightlifter-looking fellow with a buzz cut put a new filter in the coffee machine. Maybe the guy's short hair was his way around the manager's Brylcreem rules.

In the employees' lounge, Jimmy punched in his time card. Another guy came in and tossed a sack lunch into the fridge.

Crud! He'd forgotten to grab something to eat; and today he had to go straight from work to his accounting class. It would be a long day.

Back in the showroom, the powerlifter dude walked like his feet were too small for his body. "Dippity-Do Boy," he yelled, "team huddle."

With a knot in his gut, Jimmy joined the group of guys in the center of the black-and-white tiled showroom. It didn't take more than a couple of glances at his new coworkers to see he'd been had. Shaggy, un-gelled hair abounded. Heat rose in his face. Vance was just like the Lewiston manager—hazing the new guy.

"James King here has been transferred from our Lewiston store," Vance said.

"I go by Jimmy." He nodded, meeting a few gazes.

"James will work the first bay. Nice hair, by the way," Vance said, and then addressed the weightlifter, "you'll be on the floor."

Jimmy and his new boss were the only two sporting Brylcreem. He'd hear about this for months.

"Our sales goal today is to beat yesterday." Holding up his thumb, Vance peered at the notes written across his palm in blue ink. "I want five thousand by six o'clock."

"Come on, yesterday was a record," moaned a shaggy redhead.

"A record for the month and the fair's just started." Vance held an open hand to the middle, and they all joined in.

"One, two, three . . . team!"

Back at the Lewiston store, they yelled *Bill's*. Things were different here.

"Quite a few zombies here this morning." Matt nodded toward the front windows where a handful of customers stood peering through the glass.

They didn't officially open until eight o'clock.

On his way to the outside bay, Jimmy caught Vance's attention. "Do I have to wear this all day?" He pointed to his greased hair.

"Only if you want to be on my good side."

He shouldn't have asked.

Using the air gun, Jimmy changed out the wheels on a four-door Chevy coupe. There was a steady flow of customers and cars. Comparable to the night before, his tummy was again mildly upset. Fortunately, he wasn't working the floor. In the open-air bay, he could time the use of his air gun with his cinnamon blasts.

"Goodyear," Dave, the shaggy redhead, said in a monotone voice.

What did he mean . . . *Goodyear*? Bill's didn't carry the well-known tire brand.

"Goodyear," another one of the guys said.

Jimmy glanced over his shoulder. A cute brunette crossed the parking lot toward the showroom. Sunlight dappled her hair. He stared; jaw slack, gripping the air gun tighter so he wouldn't drop it on his foot. The double doors closed behind her as she exited his dream.

He blinked and went back to work.

The code word for "cute girl" at the Lewiston location had simply been *Radial*. The code for "not so cute" was *Spare,* and, unfortunately, every female under one-hundred years of age was rated.

"Ninety-nine." It wasn't so much the number that grabbed Jimmy's ear, but the monotone note in Dave's voice.

"Ninety-nine," reverberated through the bay.

A heavy-set older woman employing a cane entered the showroom.

"James King," Vance yelled from the doorway, "your turn on the floor."

Jimmy finished the final step of tightening the lug nuts by hand until the torque wrench clicked. And, then he wiped his hands on a shop rag, before entering the showroom.

"We're slammed. How are you with selling?" Vance asked.

"Fine, sure." Jimmy glanced to the reception area and nodded toward the heavy-set woman. It was a test of some type. Maybe she was Bill's wife or someone's kin. Everything was a test for the new guy.

"Fourteen . . ." Vance called the ticket number for the next customer.

It wasn't Mrs. Ninety-nine, but *Miss Goodyear* who rose from her chair and approached the counter.

Jimmy swallowed. *This is a test . . . of the emergency broadcast system. This is only a test.*

"I'm Jimmy, how may I help you?" The gal was five-five, maybe five-six, lean, and very attractive. Miss Goodyear had to be a setup. Out of the corner of his eye, he saw Matt pour himself a cup of coffee in the reception area.

"Hi. I'm getting two new tires for my aunt's car. She wants quality." The young woman held up a white recipe card with a list of instructions on it.

"Is the car here?"

"Yes."

"Let's go take a look at it." He strode ahead of her and held open the right side of the glass double doors.

"It's the white Ford Taurus." She nodded toward an older sedan in a parking space out front.

As they strolled across the blacktop parking lot, the shop noise dropped several decibels. He did a visual check of all the tires before he crouched down near the driver's side rear wheel and checked the tire specs. Like Braille, the letters were raised off the surface of the sidewall.

"The tread's getting bare on these back two, so it's a good thing she's taking care of it before winter." He dusted off his hands and tried to keep his pending flatulence at bay as they headed back inside.

"Can I take a look at that?" he asked, nodding to the little white card. She handed it to him, and he studied her aunt's requirements as they strode through the showroom, and took a right at the second row of tires on display.

The girl was cute, pleasant, family oriented. He wondered if she liked country music. Too bad she hadn't told him her name.

Be professional. No, be very professional.

Jimmy leaned a hand against a tire in the upper row. "These Michelins are all-weather radials. They have great traction in the snow, perfect for Moscow winters." He glanced from her vibrant hazel eyes to the recipe card that was presently his brain. "They have a 500,000-mile warranty and are a great deal." He shook his head. "I mean 5,000, 50,000-mile warranty."

Her cheeks inverted.

The showroom felt too quiet.

"How much are they? She's on a fixed income." Her gaze rose from his eyes to take in his Fonzie-style hair.

His stomach knotted up bad.

"Uh . . . for the pair, it will be $129.00 before tax. So, with seven percent sales tax . . ." He shifted his feet a bit, studying the fluorescent lighting. "She's looking round about $140.00."

"And they're the best deal you have for the money?"

"Yes, ma'am." He could not move. Oh, no, it was a silent one, which meant it was deadly. They had to move . . . now.

He started for the front counter.

"I'll give her a call, just to make sure she's okay with it."

"That's great," he said as another silent one escaped him. Please don't breathe. Everyone had told him that living with Grandma Ethel was going to prove memorable for him. That he'd have stories to tell. And it was only his second day.

He turned the phone to face Miss Goodyear and moved a few steps away while she dialed her aunt's number and told her about the deal.

There was only the tiniest hint of odor, and she could easily think it was Vance.

Miss Goodyear held the receiver out toward him. "My aunt wants to ask you a few questions."

He held it to his ear. "This is Jimmy. How may I help you?" He set an elbow on the counter. Some of the crew appeared to be standing around watching.

"Hello, young man, is this your very best deal for quality tires?"

She almost sounded like Mrs. Wooten, Grandma's neighbor.

"Yes, ma'am, it is." While he spoke, he grabbed a current ad off the counter and flipped through it, confirming his answer. "For the money, they are a solid value, plus they come with road hazard coverage. They're an all-weather tire. Sleet, snow… if you were ever to have an issue with them, any one of our six Bill's locations would back up their *50,000*-mile road warranty." He glanced at the girl.

She was looking toward the windows.

"Thank you. Please put Bridget back on."

Bridget. Miss Goodyear's name was *Bridget.* He handed her the receiver, grinning.

"Thanks, James. I'll take it from here." Vance reached for a clipboard.

"Jimmy," he said, under his breath.

He was at the bottom of the totem pole again.

"Thank you for your business, ma'am." He glanced toward Bridget.

"Thank you." She briefly lifted her gaze.

He headed for the bay, and through the steel door's upper window saw that a Ford half-ton had replaced the earlier rig he'd been working on. Opening the door, a torrential wave of cold water doused him from above.

"Awh . . .!" He grit his teeth, chilled to the bone.

The outside crew bellowed in unison. "Welcome to Bill's Tires of Moscow."

He shook himself off and peered overhead to where Dave stood in the upper rafters, holding a yellow five-gallon bucket and grinning. Initiating the new help was a tradition that evidently ran deep through the tire store chain.

After a few hollers and pats on the back, everyone returned to work.

The only reason he'd had the privilege of working the showroom with Bridget was to get the bucket brigade ready. She wasn't a test or staged or kin.

Jimmy grinned.

Chapter Five

"Ethel, it's Sandy. I hope I didn't catch you at a bad time." She must be calling to check on Jimmy.

"No, not at all." Ethel pressed the phone closer to her ear. "Wait a second; I can barely hear you. The dishwasher's on."

After she turned off the noisy machine, Ethel stretched the phone cord so she could look out the picture window above her dining table. Across the street, Joyce's white sedan backed out of her gravel driveway. She was on her way to the fair, probably in a hurry to see what primary- colored ribbon she'd won this year. Ethel was in no hurry to see whatever secondary-colored ribbon she herself had received. If she'd received one at all.

"Jimmy's always been good about keeping the peace around here," Sandy said. "Jorie and Jacob are already squabbling more."

"Hopefully, things will iron themselves out." Ethel sat down in a chair at the table. "Jimmy started his first day of work this morning, and then he has school this afternoon. I'm sure enjoying his company."

"As you know, he was more moldable than the first two." Her daughter-in-law sighed.

Sighing was always Sandy's way of preparing her for bad news. Senses alert, Ethel waited.

"You don't happen to know if Allison has visited yet?"

"No, not that I'm aware of." Not unless Jimmy had jerry-rigged a ladder to the dormer window. Ethel glanced toward the front yard. "Isn't she his old girlfriend?"

"According to her parents, Allison's looking for a place to live in Moscow. She's started a little company, and she can pretty much take it with her."

"Oh, what kind of business?"

"T-shirts. She does cute little sayings and designs. I'm not sure how Jimmy will feel about Allison following him."

Ethel had known things were too good to be true. "Is she a psycho, Sandy?"

"No-oo." Her daughter-in-law laughed.

Sandy was usually so serious. She probably didn't have time to laugh, as she was always running the kids around, working part-time to make ends meet, making the kids' lunches...

Ethel's heart stopped. "Sandy, Jimmy didn't take a lunch with him today."

"It's time he starts figuring out his own lunches. Heaven knows, Ethel, I've spoiled him far too long."

Wow, Sandy had been making his lunches for a long time. Ethel couldn't help but feel bad that she hadn't at least asked him. "The boss has him working a split shift, and he won't get home from work until after six today. I better run something over to him."

"According to Michael, we can't be enablers. Ethel, this will be a lesson for him. He won't forget the next time. The second reason I've called is, when Jimmy grabbed his pile of paperwork off the counter, I think he grabbed our Visa bill. I need to pay it soon. Could you ask him to look for it when he's home? Maybe write him a note, so you don't forget? I'm afraid we're getting close to the due date."

"Oh, you don't want to be late on your payment. I'll go check his room right now and call you back."

"Would you? That'd be great." Her daughter-in-law's anxious sigh only confirmed how important it was for her to do this.

Ethel held on to the handrail as she climbed the steep stairwell to Jimmy's room. She didn't care what Sandy said; she was going to make Jimmy a lunch and take it to him. He wouldn't be home until dinnertime; and with all of his tire slinging, he'd be hungry. If he were anything like her, he wouldn't be able to think without food.

Upstairs, the bed was nicely made. A made bed always helped the room look presentable. "Thank you, God, for such a wonderful young man." Of course, she kept a blind eye to the pile of clothes on the floor. She leaned over to run a hand along the top of the log cabin quilt. Over twenty years ago, she'd started it for her and Edwin's thirtieth wedding anniversary. Its incompleteness was a sign that life had given her way too many hobbies.

On top of the waterfall dresser sat a stack of paperwork. Ethel turned on the brass lamp on top of the nightstand, then she sat down on the edge of the bed and flipped the pile of paperwork over, starting with the bottom first. There was the Visa bill. She set it off to one side and flipped the pile right-side up. Near the top, a cream-colored piece of stationery with large print caught her eye. Across the top was scribbled: *Baby, don't brake me.*

It sounded like a title for a love song or a car commercial.

She pulled it to the top of the pile. An outline of a coffee cup stain marred the page, and so did a lot of scribbling.

Outside, a car drove by on Logan Street, and off in the distance someone was mowing their lawn. Otherwise, her home and little neighborhood were quiet as Ethel read.

When I see the moon lite

It remidse me when we met
Fase to fase.

Despite Jimmy's terrible spelling, she continued reading.

I'll never forget
That day we met
When I saw your fase.
I thot in my minde
If you become mine
Baby don't brake me.
Baby don't brake me.
And that day I wished to see
You agen and when
I saw you with another guy
It made me want to cry.
It made me so mad and so sad.
I wanted to punch him in the eye
But I did'nt because I'm a nice guy
But when you saw me walking away
You tride to tell me that you were just friends
I did'nt lisen
And I ternd around
And walke'd away
And that made you say
Ok were throu.
Baby don't brake me.

"Whew!" Ethel covered her mouth with one hand. Hopefully, he wasn't majoring in English or stenography. Lawyers probably needed to know how to spell, too, but in her day, they'd gotten by with a lot of dictation. Most likely, whatever field Jimmy pursued, he was going to need to know how to spell. It was amazing that he'd already earned his AA, but junior colleges were notorious for being easy.

Maybe she should talk to Mike Morrison, the president of the U of I, about getting Jimmy a tutor. If Mike didn't know someone personally, he'd at least have an idea.

Ethel read through the piece again. She sure hoped Jimmy didn't want to become a songwriter.

God said there was a purpose to everything that happened. Maybe Jimmy's spelling was the reason he didn't get enough financial aid. God wanted him to live with her. Jimmy needed her, and by golly, if he wasn't going to sling tires for the rest of his life, he was going to need to learn how to spell.

She reached for the phone on Jimmy's nightstand and dialed her daughter-in-law's number.

"Sandy, I found the Visa bill. I'll pop it into the mail to you today."

"That would be great."

"I have a question. How long ago was Jimmy and Allison's breakup?"

"A couple of months. Jimmy's not very good about the breakup part, and . . . Allison has a way of showing up like a . . ."

"An old raccoon?" Ethel offered.

"No, I was thinking more along the lines of cheesecake, when you're trying to diet."

"Oh, in a good way." Ethel giggled.

"Jimmy's at the point in his life where he doesn't know what he wants to do next. Career-wise or girlfriend." Sandy sighed. "In the meantime, we all love Allison."

Ethel felt enormously relieved. Had she and Sandy ever talked like this—sharing things of the heart? Jimmy's living with her had already brought an answer to an unspoken prayer.

"Oh, and Sandy, I found what I think is a song. It was poking out the top of the pile. Has Jimmy always had a problem with spelling?"

"Years ago he did, maybe in fourth grade. He's much better than he used to be."

"He is? Wow!" Ethel rubbed the back of her neck. It was hard to imagine.

Throughout the rest of Jimmy's shift, a majority of their female patrons were labeled Ninety-nine, with very few Goodyears.

"Ninety-nine," reverberated around the bay.

It was pure luck that Jimmy looked up from the tire he was mounting. The elderly woman walking toward the front doors was Grandma, wearing one of her wide-brimmed gardening hats.

"Sorry, guys, this one's a Goodyear." He set the air gun down and jogged out of the bay. "Grandma." He halted between her and the showroom's double doors.

"You forgot your lunch, honey." She held up a brown paper bag. "I know you go from here to school and, I didn't want you running out of brain fuel."

He managed a smile. "Thanks, Grandma. I thought you'd be at the fair."

"I'm on my way there now." She sighed uneasily. "How have you been feeling, honey?"

Her question was in regards to the cinnamon blasts. There had been mild turbulence. Should he divulge the truth?

"I was afraid you were going to say that." She shook her head. He hadn't said a thing. "I had to take Tums this morning."

"Everything's going to be fine, Grandma. It'll all work out. It always does." He patted her shoulder. "I better get back to work." He ran backward for a couple of steps. "Thanks, again."

"We wouldn't want you to get fired on your first day." She waved and, thankfully, she didn't kiss her fingertips and flutter them this time.

Inside the shop, he set his lunch on the nearest counter.

"Forget your lunch, honey?" One of the guys did an old lady impression.

"Did she bring ya any cookies?" another one spouted.

"Grandma Cookies."

Jimmy tried to ignore the chuckles and jabs that reverberated through the four bays. He knew from experience the best way to handle the guys' taunting was to embrace it.

"What can I say?" He held his arms out at his sides. "She's the best grandma in the whole world." While they chuckled, he watched the brake lights of her red Chevy Nova flash before she merged into traffic. Having Grandma deliver lunch on his first day of work was the ultimate lesson. He'd never forget his lunch again.

Chapter Six

Silver? What did a silver ribbon mean? Head tilted to one side, Ethel readjusted her glasses and stared at the large ribbon taped to her plate of cinnamon rolls. She'd been hoping for a sixth-place green ribbon, but instead, she got this.

What did the large ribbon mean? In the center of the rosette-like pendant, *Best of Show* was printed in gold lettering. She'd never heard of a silver ribbon. Maybe the judges knew somehow that she was a senior.

Best of Show?

"Ethel," Joyce's gravelly voice sounded all too near. "I earned third place again, same as last year. How did your rolls fare?"

Not knowing what to make of her ribbon, Ethel stepped away from the table to let Joyce have a gander.

Eyes wide behind her gold-framed glasses, Joyce turned to stare at her. "Did you use the Rhodes dough?"

"No! You told me not to."

"There has to be some kind of mistake!" Jaw slack, Joyce studied her. "Did you cheat?"

"You know me better than that."

"Do I? The Ethel King that I know can't bake a boxed cake. Ethel King," Joyce's voice rose loud enough for everyone in the entire baked goods section to hear, "you cheated!"

The temperature rose in the old building as people turned to stare.

It wasn't the first-time Ethel had been accused of something she hadn't done. The youngest of three girls, she'd had years of practice holding her own, and she could when she had a mind to. And though she wanted to rally a battle cry like what she'd seen on the previews for "Braveheart," God took this most inopportune time to remind her of a phrase that had been planted decades deeper in her soul.

Love thy neighbor, the soft voice said. *Love thy neighbor.*

"I didn't cheat," Ethel whispered. She gripped her hands in front of her while the corners of her eyes warmed. "I prayed. I prayed..." She paused for a moment, trying to remember what her prayer had been. "I prayed that He would make my mistakes providentially delicious."

"What do you mean your mistakes?" Joyce's mouth bunched.

"I combined two recipes, accidentally. Remember, I told you on the phone?"

Joyce turned to peer at Ethel's three-inch high golden brown rolls. The way the glaze dripped over the sides looked like art. She couldn't have dripped it any prettier, even if she'd hired Martha Stewart.

"Those are not an Ethel accident." Joyce's mouth pinched tightly. "Admit it, Ethel. You used Rhodes dough!" Hands on hips, Joyce stared at her.

"I didn't. I read the rules!" Ethel's face felt as hot as a preheated oven.

She and Joyce had finally patched things up, and now the competitive brouhaha had started all over again, and this time over a silly ribbon. The silver ribbon must be a coveted prize for Joyce's round face to be green with envy, not a good combination with her dyed red hair.

Though her neighbor had been there for her during the difficult times, it was the second-time Joyce had let her down in a golden moment. The first time had been when Ethel's first great grandchild had dared to be born before Joyce's. In everything she did, Joyce wanted to be first.

But . . . Love keeps no record of wrongs. She loved Joyce, whom God had intentionally made her neighbor.

With this awareness, Ethel thought it best to remove herself before any further damage was done. So, she found the first exit door in the Exhibitor's Hall and proceeded outside into the warm afternoon sunshine.

In the shade of a nearby hemlock tree, she sat down on a wooden bench and tried not to cry. *A friend loveth at all times.* Even when the other friend receives a large silver ribbon. In the dappled shade, Ethel took off her glasses and wiped at her eyes.

"Are you okay?"

Off to her left, stood a kind-enough looking older man. Maybe it was God, the man himself, checking in on her.

"One of my best friends just accused me of cheating." She shrugged, fiddling with the handles of her faux leather purse. "I'm just having a little woe-is-me party, and then I'll be fine."

Children walked by holding cinnamon-and-sugar-covered elephant ears and foot-long swaths of tickets, excitement plastered on their faces. Only minutes ago, she'd felt that way, too. She'd always loved the fair before today. And then, Joyce ruined it for her.

"Let me get this straight." His weathered hand gripped the top of the bench. "Your best friend accused you of cheating?"

"Yes." Over the years, she and Joyce had laughed and cried together a lot.

"Did you cheat?"

"No-oo." Ethel frowned over at him.

One gray brow arched as he regarded her.

She patted a hand to her heart, trying to console herself. "To be perfectly honest, I was tempted to cheat with Rhodes in the beginning." She reflected on her earlier feelings of discouragement. "But I knew I couldn't live with myself if I did."

"With Rhodes?" His expressive brows gathered.

"But, I didn't." Ethel patted the bench seat beside her.

He sat down near the far edge—several feet away—and, back straight, set his hands to his knees.

"Have . . . have you told your husband?" He glanced over at her.

"No." Lifting her left hand, Ethel gazed at the tiny diamonds on her wedding band. "He passed away ten years ago."

The elderly man—who probably wasn't God—nodded thoughtfully. "I think it's normal, your first relationship after your spouse has passed on, to feel like you're being unfaithful. But our vows are only until death do us part."

Staring at the stranger, Ethel did a mental rewind. "Oh, no!" She sank her teeth into the sides of her cheeks and patted her heart. "No, no, no. You misunderstood me." She giggled. "My good friend and neighbor accused me of cheating because she thought I'd used Rhodes dough for my cinnamon rolls. I was going to use the store-bought dough before Joyce set me straight and had me read the rules. You see," Ethel did the little bunny ear quote, "everything has to be from scratch."

"Oh . . . I understand now." His smile deepened the lines in his tan face. The man was farmer lean, with absolutely no flab or sag beneath his chin. She wondered if the malady was something only elderly women struggled with.

"You don't happen to know the significance behind a large silver ribbon?"

"I do. I'm one of the judges for horticulture. A silver ribbon means that the entry won a blue-ribbon in one of the categories in the first round. And—"

"A blue-ribbon?" Jaw slack, she stared at him.

"Yes." He nodded. "And, in the final round—when only the blue-ribbon winners are judged—a silver is awarded for the second best of the show."

Ethel's eyes blinked before everything around them went hazy—the Ferris Wheel, the squealing children, the cotton candy mobile. "Second best of the show…?" Her belly shook as she giggled.

"Yes, you heard me correctly." The corner of his mouth twitched.

The fancy ribbon wasn't a decadent senior booby prize. It was second best of the show. *Oh, Lord, you heard my prayer.*

"Oh, my." All these years of participating in the fair, and she'd only focused on the primary colors. No wonder Joyce was green. The moment *was* golden.

Ethel felt the sun shine warm upon her. Stardust sparkled in the air, reminding her of the time when she'd first learned that Edwin King liked her. She'd been seventeen, and his sister had told her in the school library, a crowded place where one was supposed to be quiet. Ethel had stolen away and locked herself in the custodian's closet so she could giggle and embrace the news.

Her cinnamon rolls—Ethel King's cinnamon rolls—had won blue and silver ribbons at the fair. For her companion's sake, she tried to stifle her exuberance, but it couldn't be squelched. Her older sister Gladys would never believe it. Her mother, eight years in heaven, would never believe it. Edwin bless his heart, would never believe it either. She didn't believe it herself.

Lifting her glasses, she wiped at the corners of her eyes and sniffled.

"You're very fine—I mean kind—to be the deliverer of such news." Horrified by her slip, she wanted to cover her face with both hands, but instead, she inhaled bravely.

Good air in. Bad air out. She practiced Betty's mantra for stress.

The elderly man beside her blinked thoughtfully. Then his steady gaze took in her wide-brimmed gardening hat with its green-and-white ribbon knotted beneath her chin before it settled on her eyes. The look set her back fifty-some years and made her feel disoriented.

She rose from the bench. "Goodbye," she managed politely and hoped his eyes wouldn't follow her. As she walked away, she tugged on the hem of her tangerine-colored T-shirt, the one that Joyce had puff-painted the sunflowers right across the chest area, and without looking back, returned inside the Exhibitor's Hall.

Maybe the silver ribbon had been a mistake. Maybe it had been placed next to her cinnamon rolls by accident instead of Joyce's. Or . . . Ethel's brain stewed with all the possibilities.

Though Joyce was nowhere in sight, Ethel expected her to swoop in like a vulture and squawk, "Rhodes dough! Rhodes dough!"

Thank heaven she hadn't cheated and used the store-bought dough like she'd been tempted to. Ethel stared at the silver ribbon taped to her plate. It was still there. It hadn't been a mistake.

As soon as she got home, she'd call Gladys and tell her the remarkable news, even though her older sister would have to see it to believe it.

"Are you Ethel King?" A plump woman, a little younger than herself, with a strict bun, approached her.

"Yes, I am." Ethel pushed her glasses higher up the bridge of her nose and in one glance read the woman's badge: Baked Goods Judge. Joyce had turned her in for a crime that she hadn't committed.

"I'm Marlene Flanagan." The woman touched her arm. "I loved your rolls."

"Oh, thank you." Ethel felt her shoulders relax.

"They were the judges' favorite, but during the final round, one of our judges determined that the wonderful sourdough flavor was unaccounted for in your recipe."

"Judges' favorite?" Ethel blinked hard.

"Yes. Had you fully disclosed your recipe, your rolls could very well have earned the Gold."

"The Best of Show?" Ethel nodded now, piecing it all together.

"Yes, the Grand Champion. For the past three years, I've been working on a cookbook called Latah County Blue-ribbon Recipes," Marlene Flanagan said. "And with your permission, I would love to include your recipe. It was outstanding."

"It's uh, a secret-family-recipe that I cannot . . . divulge." Ethel suppressed a smile.

"I hate hearing that." The woman paused, and then her eyes widened. "Excuse me," she said. Stepping aside, she headed in the direction of the nearest exit door.

"The grand champion," Ethel marveled, fanning her face.

The woman was gone for the length of a car commercial before Ethel noted her return.

"As I was saying, Ethel, most of the recipes in this book are deemed secret-family-recipes. Each contributor will receive a free autographed copy."

"Really!" For a moment, she imagined her name *Ethel King* featured under a blue-ribbon recipe. The thought though tempting, meant she'd have to divulge the key ingredient: Soured whipping cream, a week past the shelf date, and left open in the fridge for at least five days.

"I'd better not," Ethel said, remembering the side effects.

"And why is that?" The woman shifted her feet a bit.

The conversation felt a bit pressing.

"It's a family secret that I cannot share." Ethel zipped two fingers across her lips for emphasis.

"I'm sorry to interrupt, ladies," it was the elderly man from outside, "but I was hoping to show… this… uh, young woman some horticulture." He took Ethel by the elbow and steered her toward the exit.

"Young?" She giggled, embarrassed to the core.

"I don't know your name and silver was the only other word that came to mind, and it didn't sound right."

She giggled.

Why had he saved her? Was he a stalker of some kind, parading as a gentle, old man?

"I'm sorry"—he patted her arm—"You looked very uncomfortable. Was that Joyce or did I misread the situation?"

"No, you rescued me." Ethel suppressed another giggle and waved her free hand. "Thank you. I don't even know your name." And she realized he didn't know hers either. "Mine's Ethel."

"Don Gardner. I was hoping to show you the difference between a gold-ribbon rose and a silver-ribbon rose."

Don Gardner. No wonder he liked horticulture.

Don Juan Gardner was in the midst of patting her arm that was tucked up in his as they strolled past Joyce, seated on a bench near the exit.

"That woman who just stared at us is obviously someone you know."

"Yes, that was Joyce."

"Your neighbor who accused you of cheating?"

"Yes, my neighbor and good friend."

"Then who was the woman I just rescued you from?"

"A judge who wants my recipe for her book."

"And from the looks of it, I'd say you declined her?" He peered over his shoulder at her. Curiosity in his pale blue eyes.

"Yes, it's a guarded family secret."

"Ethel . . . Ethel King," Joyce yelled. Too bad Ethel had told Don her name. Otherwise, they could have kept walking.

Instead, he retained her arm and swiveled them around to face Joyce.

Her friend looked old, lonely, and though the woman was a meticulous housekeeper and had been a white-ribbon baker six years running, she needed a professional to do her hair.

"Yes, Joyce?"

"You've often raved about the cinnamon rolls from that little café in Potlatch."

"Ireland's Café? *Raved* is the wrong word. I've never even had one. And, I've recently been corrected. They're sticky buns, not cinnamon rolls."

"Is that what you did, Ethel? Did you frost some of Ireland's sticky buns?"

The accusation was ridiculous and in front of her new friend. She tried to swivel Don Gardner back around, but he'd pinned her elbow.

"I know you can't bake, Ethel. Only last month you said you weren't going to enter the fair unless they had a Dump

Cake category. And yesterday morning, you were thawing Rhodes dough in your microwave." Joyce's eyes bulged behind her wire-framed glasses. "And today, you've won the blue, and for *taste*."

Taste! That's what she'd won the blue in? Oh, bless those judges' taste buds!

"You know that was before I read the rules," Ethel finally countered.

"You can't bake, but you can earn a Best of Show?" Joyce's voice wavered.

Ethel clamped down on the inside of her cheeks.

Love thy neighbor. The soft voice said a little louder now. *Love thy neighbor.*

"Joyce, you and I only fight when we're at the fair. Next year, let's do our friendship a favor and not enter the same category."

With her mouth pinched tight, Joyce glanced at Ethel's escort. "I was only going to enter my dinner rolls, and then Virginia inspired me. But, you're right, Ethel." Joyce's chest rose and deflated as she sighed. "It was such a shock seeing your name, you, of all people, with that grand ribbon attached. Why, if I ever won that honor," her good friend's chin bunched, "I'd pin it right here," she patted above her heart, "have my picture taken and send it out as my Christmas card."

"I know," Ethel said, softly, "and someday you will, Joyce. You're too good of a baker."

Joyce's shoulders slackened, and her countenance softened. Then before her neighbor could say another word, Don spun them a hundred and eighty-degree turn, and they started for the exit door.

Flatulence was the true fruit of her labor, that and the second best of show ribbon, of course. Ethel vowed to herself that someday she'd tell Joyce the truth, but not today.

Not in front of Don Gardner.

Chapter Seven

"Goodnight, Edwin." Ethel flung a kissed finger toward his picture on the nearby nightstand. Instead of turning out the lamp, she gazed at his handsome face and felt the years slip away. The picture had been taken of him in his navy-blue sailor's uniform in the same year they'd been wed, 1951.

"Remember the cinnamon rolls that I told you about? Well, I won a silver ribbon for second-Best of Show at the fair. Me, of all people." She chewed her lower lip and let it uncurl.

"I made a friend today. Don. And, he's just a friend. You'd like him. He's a gentleman.

"Not that you weren't. Except I still wish you wouldn't have smoked your cigars in the house. Other than that, you were my best friend." She sighed, missing him. "It's funny, Eddy, how you're only a memory away." Tears surfaced for a moment before she blinked them aside. And, then she leaned forward and turned off the lamp.

Monday morning after Jimmy left for school, Ethel dialed Quinn's cell phone number and invited her granddaughter's boyfriend over for meatloaf.

"What can I bring?" Quinn asked.

"Just bring yourself and one tomato, if you have any left."

"Myself and one tomato. Ethel, I'll look forward to it all day."

"I will, too. It'll be just like old times." After she hung up, she said a prayer that Katherine's move to Potlatch wouldn't hurt Quinn and her granddaughter's relationship. For the next semester, seventeen miles and Moscow Mountain separated the two love birds.

That evening the savory smell of meatloaf wafted through Ethel's bungalow on Logan Street. Instead of running the fan above the stove, she went about the house fluffing curtains and opening linen drawers and all of her closets in the hope that the smell would overrule Edwin's lingering cigar smoke.

When she returned to the kitchen, Jimmy and Quinn were already seated at the table, conversing. No introductions on her part were required.

She set the Fiestaware bowl full of mashed potatoes on the table between the loaf pan of saucy meatloaf and a bowl of steaming green beans. A plate of sliced Roma tomatoes was Quinn's contribution. Not your average bachelor fare, if she did say so herself.

"Did Grandma tell you that she won second best of the show for her cinnamon rolls?" Jimmy asked.

"That's right. Katherine told me. Congratulations, Ethel."

"I prayed that the Lord would make them providentially delicious." Ethel felt her face warm before she sat down in her usual chair.

"Are any of your cinnamon rolls left, Grandma?"

"Yes. I hid a few from you in the fridge. We'll heat them up and have them for dessert, unless, of course, Quinn has another social engagement this evening." She kicked Jimmy's shin beneath the table.

"I don't." Quinn shook his head.

"Good." Ethel gripped the men's hands for prayer. "Our Dear Heavenly Father, thank you for Your Son Jesus and His sacrifice. Thank you for the wonderful meatloaf recipe that my friend Betty gave me. Watch over Katherine and Jimmy with their new jobs, and Quinn with his job, too. In Your Son's name, we pray, Amen."

"Isn't Potlatch only sixteen miles?" Jimmy asked.

Quinn nodded as he loaded a spoonful of mashed potatoes onto his plate.

"Why didn't Katherine just stay here and commute?" Jimmy scooped a serving of green beans onto his plate.

"Because she's a tightwad," Ethel interjected. "I told her she could drive Edwin's old truck, but that meant she'd have to pay for insurance, gas, and a few other things."

"The teacher who's on maternity leave is an old friend of hers from the U of I, and offered her free housing—a tiny, one-room cabin on their property." Quinn unfolded his napkin over his lap.

"Katherine only has to pay for electricity. It's an adventure for her," Ethel added, though she didn't understand why she needed an adventure with Quinn so fresh on the line.

Jimmy tipped back his head, downing half a glass of milk.

"And . . ." Ethel wagged a finger. "She's not keen on the idea of driving over Moscow Mountain twice a day in the winter." Which would have been an adventure for Katherine, but instead of mentioning that, Ethel savored her first bite of meatloaf. If there'd been a meatloaf category at the Latah County Fair, she would have entered this recipe.

"Grandma, Mrs. Wooten drives a white Ford Taurus, doesn't she?" Jimmy asked, out of the blue.

"I'm not sure. It is white . . . with four doors?"

"She thought my Volvo was a Buick," Quinn informed Jimmy across the length of the table. "One time when I rolled up, she thought I was the paperboy."

Ethel giggled. "Edwin used to tell me 'just because it has four doors doesn't make it a Buick.'"

The two men laughed.

"Well . . ." Jimmy smiled, "I think I spoke with Mrs. Wooten on the phone at the shop last week."

"Joyce said something about wanting new tires." Ethel savored another bite of meatloaf.

Quinn patted the table between them, his ebony eyes unusually bright. "Did Katherine tell you that she's decided to apply for her doctorate?"

"No-oo!" She stared at him. "That didn't take her very long."

"Throughout grad school, Evans encouraged her to pursue her Ph.D. All it took was three weeks of being back in a high school classroom." Quinn shook his head. "She's having an issue with discipline."

"Of course, she is. Most teens don't like history or discipline." Ethel sighed.

The phone rang in the other room.

"Could you get that for me?" Ethel patted the corner of the table between her and Jimmy. It was probably for him anyways. All of her friends knew better than to call at dinnertime.

"Sure." Jimmy rose and grabbed it before the third ring.

Ph.D. Wow! After this semester, Katherine might be living with her again, or would she and Quinn be married by then? She studied the smile in his handsome profile.

"I'll get her for you, Don." Jimmy's voice carried into her white, boxy kitchen.

Don? Ethel rose from the table. Who did she know named Don? Halfway to the phone, she halted in her tracks.

Don Juan Gardner.

Holding out the phone, Jimmy eyed her with furrowed brows. Ethel forced herself to continue toward him and take the receiver from his grip. While he returned to the table, she lifted it to her ear.

From Baked Goods, Don had escorted her to the Horticulture Building, where he'd shown her the difference between Second Best of Show roses and the Grand Champions. To her amateur eye, the only difference had been the ribbons.

"Hel-lo." Her voice cracked.

"Hello, Ethel, it's Don. Don Gardner . . . from the fair." She stared in the mirror above her curio cabinet. Her bobbed, mousy gray hair needed a beautician, maybe a magician.

"Yes, hello." When he'd first seen her, she'd been wearing her gardening hat. Her wide-brimmed straw hat had probably been what had first drawn him to her.

"There aren't a lot of Kings in the phone book. Did you know that your husband's name is still listed in the . . ." a rustling sound followed, "2002 directory?"

On the phone, he had a matter-of-fact way about him, like Mildred.

"I like it that way. When your name's Ethel, everyone knows you're an old lady. And . . . not very many old ladies, I know, want everyone in Latah County to be informed that they live alone. Not that I live alone, my grandson is here now. He attends the university and works at Bill's Tires." She stopped herself from rambling on into forever.

"I see. Well, Ethel, you mentioned that your roses have aphids. I do have some of that insecticide left that I was telling you about. It's all natural, and won't harm any of your nearby shrubbery."

"Oh . . . that's great." A giggle escaped her. He wasn't calling for a date. He only wanted to spray her roses.

"What's a good morning for me to stop by? It's always best to spray in the morning. As you may already know, a wet rose picks up mold."

Hmm . . . the girls were coming over on Thursday for Scrabble, so it was best she get him out of the way as soon as possible. "Tomorrow's fine. Any time after eight." She wanted to make sure Jimmy was off to school before Don Gardner's Aphid Service stopped by.

"I'll see you tomorrow then, my dear."

My dear? Ethel locked eyes with herself in the mirror.

A clunkity, clunk crashing sound followed before the line went dead.

"Oh, dear." She gulped. Maybe Don had more on his mind than insecticide. She inhaled deeply and returned to the table.

"Who was that, Grandma?" Jimmy turned to watch her.

"Just a man." She waved a hand.

"A man?" Jimmy grinned and glanced across the table at Quinn.

"He's coming over tomorrow to spray my roses. I . . . I have an aphid problem." She didn't look at either of them as she returned the paper napkin to her lap.

"An exterminator?" Quinn asked. Leaning back in his chair, he glanced past her to the clock on the stove.

"For a second there, we thought you might have an admirer," Jimmy said. "Don almost sounded nervous on the phone. 'Is... Ethel, uh, Ethel King there?'"

She hadn't noticed his nervous inflection when she'd been on the phone, maybe because she'd been out-of-sorts herself.

"Just an exterminator," Jimmy said, reaching for a second scoop of mashed potatoes. "And we thought Quinn had something fun to tell Katherine."

Ethel chuckled along with her grandson and avoided glancing to her right at Quinn's side of the table.

"What's the name of the exterminator company?" Quinn scooped his second slice of meatloaf from the pan.

Didn't he believe her?

"Ladies with the name of Ethel can't be too careful nowadays." His Zhivago eyes narrowed.

"It's uh . . ." Her gaze roved the white cotton valance with embroidered strawberries framing the top of the window. "Uh... Gardner's Aphid Service."

It was only a tiny white lie.

"Wow, specialized." Jimmy grinned.

With his dark brows gathered, Quinn studied her.

"Yes. And what I like about it is . . ." She blinked, trying to remember Don's wording. "It's all natural, and won't harm any of my nearby shrubbery."

"Something's amiss." Quinn tapped his fingers on the corner of the table between them. "Why did he have to look you up in the directory? Those types of services usually already have your number."

"Well, they didn't. That's why he . . . *they* . . . had to look up my number." Heat climbed her neck. If Quinn pried any further, she'd forfeit her cinnamon roll and let him eat two. She clamped down on her cheeks at the thought.

"You're trying not to smile about something, Ethel."

"I'm happy, that's all. It's not every day I have two of my favorite men in all of the world here for meatloaf."

"And an admirer call." Quinn eyed her smugly.

Good air in. Bad air out.

Just for that, she'd serve him *two* of her prizewinning cinnamon rolls.

Chapter Eight

For her eight o'clock aphid meeting with Don Gardner, Ethel wore her regular gardening clothes—elastic waistband pants and her coral-colored T-shirt that Sharon had puff painted pansies across the front. She wouldn't dress up for Don. This was not a date.

During breakfast, Jimmy squirted Reddi-Wip over his coffee.

"How's your tummy feeling?" Ethel asked, and waited for him to say, "Poor Quinn."

"Now that your cinnamon rolls are gone, Grandma"— Jimmy scanned the table—"a better name for them would have been Cinnamon Blasts." He grinned like she was supposed to find this humorous.

Those poor judges had no idea that her blue and silver-ribbon rolls had been the reason behind their frantic search for the EXIT doors.

"Poor Quinn," Jimmy finally said.

Ethel nodded. He'd savored his second cinnamon roll even more than the first.

"Do you have anything special planned today?" Jimmy asked. Whipped cream adorned his upper lip like a thin mustache.

"No. The aphid man will be here sometime this morning."

"Now, there's one job I know I don't ever want to do."

Jimmy hadn't been blessed with a light at the end of his career tunnel. Her other grandchildren that had lived with her while attending the U of I had known exactly what degree they were after, what they wanted to be when they grew up. Thomas, her oldest grandson, was now a civil engineer in Bellingham. And, then there had been Tim, who'd majored in Philanthropy, and thought he was God's gift to women. She remembered his front porch escapades—maybe he was. And then—

"Has anyone called for me?" Jimmy interrupted her musings.

"No. What time do you need to leave this morning?" He didn't seem in as big of a hurry as he'd been last week.

"My boss wants me to be at work by 7:25."

"And you work early on . . .?"

"I work nine-hour days on Tuesdays and Thursdays. Grandma . . ." Jimmy appeared thoughtful. "Have you ever known anyone who's done tile work?"

"No." Her three sons had held their share of jobs and careers, but tile work had not been among them. "Why?"

He shrugged. "Last night at work, my boss wanted me to check for loose tiles in the showroom. He had me take this toilet bowl plunger, you know, the type with a long wooden handle and the black, round suction head?"

"Yes." Ethel blinked, and setting an elbow on the table, pushed her glasses higher up the bridge of her nose.

"They call it the Tile Check." Jimmy's chest expanded as he inhaled deeply. "Anyways, I put the plunger in the center of each tile to check the suction, make sure none of them are coming loose."

Did he know he was painting a Gomer Pyle picture? It wasn't pretty.

"Were any . . . loose?" Her voice climbed an octave.

"No."

"I thought you sold tires."

"We do. Vance, my boss, had me check tiles for the last half hour or so before closing. I only got done with," he shook his head, "I dunno . . . a sixth of the store." His chest expanded. "Grandma, do you know how stupid I felt?"

"No-oo." She meant yes.

"This manager hazes the new guy a lot longer than the Lewiston branch ever did," his voice trailed off unhappily.

She was glad he'd figured this out all on his own. Turning in her chair, she glanced over her shoulder for a view of the clock on the stove. 7:10.

"This boss likes to holler. Throw his weight around. Makes you feel about this big." Jimmy held his thumb and forefinger two inches apart. "The problem is, if I want to keep this job, I'll probably be plunging tiles again tonight."

Poor Jimmy.

"Let's pray about it, honey."

He nodded and gripped her hands above the table.

"Our Dear Heavenly Father." Sometimes her prayers just flowed, but already she was drawing a blank. "What a beautiful day you've blessed us with." The morning sky was a cloudless blue. "Help Jimmy with his new job." Again, the abyss of nothingness. "We pray that he has a good work day. Help the truth to be exposed." Where did that come from? ". . . in Jesus' name, Amen."

"Sorry, honey. Sometimes my prayers flow, and sometimes there's a struggle."

"Last night when you prayed for my job," he held her gaze for a moment, and his somberness just pulled the grandma-stuffing right out of her, "it reminded me that I'm not alone."

"Oh, honey, you're never alone. Jesus walks with us. He bears our burdens."

"I know."

Plunging tiles! Why, if this Vance fellow continued to push her grandson around, she'd report his hollering and the…   tile plunging to . . . Bill, the owner!

Good air in. Bad air out.

Better yet, she'd report him to her Boss.

Wearing his dark blue work pants and short-sleeve, white button-down shirt, Jimmy made his way through the kitchen. Grandma was standing at the ready, a bagged lunch in her grip.

"Thanks, Grandma, you're the best." He kissed her forehead.

"Did you see yesterday's photo?" She nodded toward the fridge.

"No." He paused in front of the old white Frigidaire. A clunky magnet pinned yesterday's Polaroid picture to the upper door. It was the best photo ever. Instead of him leaning against the gate, Grandma had him lean against the door of his Mercury Cougar. Wow! He liked the way the sun glinted off his new paint job. He had very few pictures of him and his car.

"I love this one!" he said.

"It's my favorite, too."

"That's the first good photo I have of me with my car." He glanced at her and smiled. "Thanks, Grandma. Don't lose that one."

While he made his way down the back walk, his memory tripped to Allison, his first and only girlfriend, and the photo of the two of them together that he'd stashed somewhere. The old pinchy uncomfortable feeling returned in the center of his chest. There were a lot of things that he really liked about Allison. Maybe it was the distance; but, as of late, he was having a difficult time remembering what it was that he didn't like about her.

He swung his heavy backpack and the sack lunch to the passenger side of the bench seat, slid behind the wheel, and turned the key in the ignition.

A yellow sticky note was stuck to the middle of his rearview mirror.

His cousin Tim had only made it two days before receiving one of Grandma's sticky note sermons. Jimmy had made it six.

He scanned the west-facing windows, the side of the house, the trunk of the nearby crabapple tree, and the corner of the detached garage for his grandmother before plucking the yellow slip of paper from the mirror.

His chest concaved slightly before he read the note.

I am with you always.

- God.

P.S. I'm also your best friend.

A sense of peace washed over him. *I'm also your best friend.* He mulled over the last line, surprised that God hadn't added *and so is your grandmother.*

He stuck the note to the front of the metal ashtray. The funny thing about his first sticky note from God was it didn't feel like a sermon at all.

When he stopped at the traffic light at the intersection to the Lewiston Highway, he glanced again at the note.

I am with you always.

- God.

In their own way, God and Grandma had written exactly what he'd needed to hear.

For a little over a half hour, Ethel had her bungalow on Logan Street all to herself. While she folded a load of laundry, she realized that she hadn't told Don that she preferred her guests to park in back. She put on her gardening hat, went out front and swept the porch clear of cobwebs and dust. From there, she Windexed the windows. One chore led to another. She was still tidying the porch when Don rolled up in a gold Buick station wagon.

His car door swung open, and he stepped outside. "Good morning, Ethel." He grinned and made a slight wave above the hood of his vehicle.

"Good morning, Don." Cupping a hand above her eyes, she remained on the top step while he grabbed a squirt bottle from the back.

She glanced across the street at Joyce's front windows. Was her neighbor watching with the old pair of binoculars that Ethel had given her years ago?

Her great ideas often came back to bite her.

Don closed the gate behind him and with a bouncy step sauntered toward her. He appeared lighter on his feet than she'd remembered as if he didn't have one drop of arthritis like so many their age were hampered by. She wondered if he could hop the fence without tearing his pant cuff.

Don halted two yards away from her. "Some dear friends of mine live a block or two from here. Through the years, I've driven by your place many a time." His inflection tugged at her heart. Edwin used to say *many a time* just like Don had.

"What're your friends' names?"

"Phoebe and Stan Farkle. They live on the corner of the next block." He nodded north.

"I met Phoebe Farkle once when I delivered some homemade banana bread." Sadly, Ethel hadn't discovered that she'd forgotten the salt and something else equally important until after she'd made the delivery. Like she so often told her grandchildren, you only have one chance to make a first impression. Over a decade ago, she'd welcomed the Farkles to the neighborhood, and she'd never seen or heard from them since.

"Lead the way to these infested roses." Don's blue eyes sparkled up at her in the morning sunlight.

"I need to prepare you; they are very sad." She led the way to the front left corner of the yard. Instead of beautifying the walkway in front of her home, her tall, pink roses were miserable globs of stickiness.

"Oh, I see . . . they are prolific." He scanned the nearby shrubs. "Most likely, they've infested your other flowers."

While Don began spraying, Ethel studied her black-eyed Susans and other nearby perennials. The creepy little bugs were everywhere.

"I didn't know aphids came in pink," she said.

"They come in a variety of colors." Don seemed to know a lot about roses, bushes, bugs . . .

"My black-eyed Susans should be renamed pink-eyed Susans."

He chuckled and continued to be all business.

Maybe he wasn't here to woo her.

Little patches of red clover appeared to have cropped up overnight. While he puttered and sprayed, she returned to the porch for her handheld metal rake and bucket. Then she dug the tillers deep into the soil, trying to get the pesky roots. Hopefully, Joyce wasn't looking out her window, or she'd see her gardening with the man from the fair. Her neighbor could be a yacker. Fortunately, they knew very few people in the same circle. Except, that is, for Mike Morrison. And, there wasn't any reason for Joyce to share Ethel's personal life with the president of the U of I.

"I'm afraid you have a serious problem, Ethel." Don pulled off a glove and ran a forearm across his brow.

She peered up at him, thankful that his gaze was on the flowers, and not her.

"I hope the insecticide's not too expensive."

"It isn't." He chuckled.

Over the next half hour, he completely emptied the contents of the bottle on her front flowers. She didn't have the heart to tell him that there were equally infested roses in her side yard.

"We need to wait an hour, and then gently hose off any residue."

"An hour?" She gulped. Was this his way of getting invited inside for a cup of coffee and baked goods? If so, it was clever. Had she done her breakfast dishes? She tried to remember.

"I don't want to be a bother for you. I can spray them off." She waved a hand.

"Not at all, I enjoy helping fellow gardeners." His Adam's apple bobbed in his lean neck.

For a moment, he looked pitifully lonely, and she was reminded that he didn't have grandchildren living with him, blessing him with their company, keeping him young.

"Would you like to come in for a cup of coffee?"

"I'd love to." He glanced at his wristwatch. "But if you think you'll be fine handling the rest yourself, it'll give me a chance to catch up on some other errands."

"Oh, okay." Now, she supposed it was her turn to feel slighted. She stood near the fence in her wide-brimmed gardening hat with the soft green ribbon tied beneath her chin and watched his shiny clean Buick take a right on her little side street. The flash of his brake lights as he drove past the south side of her bungalow probably had nothing to do with him having second thoughts about coffee. Most likely, he'd spotted her other bed of pink roses in the side yard, their sticky blooms visible a foot above the fence.

Had the difference between a Grand Champion and a Second Best of Show rose simply been a line that he'd used over and over with aging beauties at the fair? She had to give him credit. If he was looking for an elderly wife with baking skills, the Baked Goods section at the fair was an excellent place to start. Except, if she were completely honest with herself, she'd met him on a bench outside the Exhibitor's Hall.

Chapter Nine

The phone rang Thursday morning right before the Scrabble girls were due to arrive.

"Hello."

"Ethel, it's Betty, I forgot to tell you that I won't be able to make it today. June and her second husband are in town. And, I told you I'd bring a cheese plate. I'm sorry for the late notice."

"That's okay, Betty. I'll call someone. Have a nice time with your daughter and son-in-law." Ethel hung up and grimaced in the mirror. "Late notice—the girls will be here any minute!"

Who could she ask in a pinch? It had to be someone who lived close. Her sister, Gladys, hated Scrabble. Jimmy was at school. Then she recalled the handwritten song of his that she'd found upstairs, "Baby, don't brake me," and the way he'd spelled again, a-g-e-n, and tried, t-r-y-d. She could never ask Jimmy.

Even though Ethel hadn't spoken with Joyce since the fair, she was her only choice.

She dialed her neighbor's number, and then stretching the phone cord, moved to the large picture window near her maple table. Mildred's brick red sedan slowly made a right onto her side street with Sharon's salt-and-pepper hair visible on the passenger side.

"Hell-o," Joyce answered.

"Joyce, it's Ethel."

"Hell-o, Ethel."

"How are you?" If Joyce had seen Don Gardner's Buick parked out front of her place or the two of them gardening together on Tuesday, she was being awfully quiet about it.

"I just got my hair done." This meant that Joyce's red hair was now curled and lacquered.

"Oh, that's nice. I have my Scrabble party starting in a few minutes, and one of our regulars isn't able to make it. I was wondering if you'd like to join us?"

The back door creaked open. Mildred entered and set a bag of Doritos on the counter. Behind her, Sharon carried in a bag of baby carrots.

"I'll be right over." The other end of the line went dead.

What a friend! Despite their rifts over the years, as soon as Ethel caved in and made the call, she and Joyce had always been able to patch things up. That was the beauty of their friendship.

"Betty won't be able to make it, but I just found a sub," she informed the girls.

"Wonderful." They bustled past her into the living room to put their purses away and use the restroom.

Their little luncheon was missing Betty's cheese plate—their protein. From an overhead cupboard, Ethel pulled down a jar of roasted peanuts. Next, she checked the fridge for eggs. There were only two. The peanuts would have to do.

Joyce soon joined their little party and set a plate of tiny, pink-colored mints leftover from her granddaughter's wedding on the counter. Today, they even had a dessert.

After introductions had been made, the foursome sat down at her table in the living room.

"So, do you live close, Joyce?" Sharon asked.

"Yes, right across the street." Joyce sat with her back to the picture window. Turning slightly in her chair, she peered over her shoulder. "See the immaculate, white house?"

"Uh-huh." Sharon, who was seated on Ethel's right, leaned toward the window.

"That's my place. Ethel and I have been neighbors for over two decades."

"We've heard about you for years," Mildred said, dryly.

Oh, why did she have to word it that way? Ethel may have vented a few too many times over the years, but never without a contrite heart.

"Joyce . . ." Sharon's gaze roved the plain white walls of the living room. "Your name sounds familiar."

A silence similar to a dead hearing aid followed.

Ethel felt her left shoulder drop a bit as she tried not to sweat.

Wide-eyed, Mildred glanced at Ethel.

"Are you a baker?" Sharon asked.

"Why, yes, I am. I'm sure you gals have heard about Ethel's success at the fair." Joyce took tiles out of the cloth bag, one letter at a time. "She may have won a higher ribbon than me in the cinnamon roll category, but I can tell you, ladies, she can't touch my sticky buns."

The dead hearing aid silence returned.

Ethel had no desire to touch her . . . um, sticky buns.

Seated to her left, Mildred eyed her over the top of her spectacles. "Aren't you going to say something?"

"I've never made sticky buns, so Joyce is right. I don't even have a recipe."

"Aren't sticky buns just cinnamon rolls with nuts?" Sharon asked.

"No-oo." Ethel shook her head.

"Pretty much." Joyce nodded. "Except you spread a caramel sauce evenly in the bottom of the pan. I always like to use my Pyrex so I can see the bubbly gooiness."

Mildred was already swallowing.

"Then you add a layer of toasted pecans. Some people like to put the pecans in first, and then the sauce. But, not me. I like to position each pecan. And, lastly, you place your shaped cinnamon rolls on top and bake to perfection."

Joyce knew how to paint a pretty picture.

Sharon set an elbow on the table and leaned into it. "It's been forever since I've had a good sticky bun."

"Joyce, you and I are partners." Ethel looked across the table at her.

"You may have to remind me."

"You'll do fine." Over the years, Ethel had received numerous cards from Joyce and knew firsthand that the woman could spell.

"Oh, for crying in the bucket." Sharon set her last letter in the rack. "I don't even have a vowel."

"Other people will. Who has an *A*?" Mildred asked.

"Ethel, didn't you say there's a luncheon?" Joyce eyed Ethel across the table.

"It's on the counter. Sometimes our potlucks are better than others,"

"That's an easy fix. Next time just tell people what to bring."

That was the problem with subs. All too often they just wanted to take over.

Joyce had the letter *A,* so she went first and right off the bat was able to spell "blank."

"Nice!" Ethel clapped her hands together and couldn't believe her luck in having her neighbor for a partner.

Instead of putting her "s" at the end of *blank* and earning twelve points for the new word, Sharon used the "a" for her vowel and spelled "Sag" for four points." At least she hadn't spelled gas forward—only backward.

An hour later, Ethel and Joyce led by eighty points.

"They're still fighting over there in Afghanistan." Mildred popped a peanut into her mouth. "Their cars and homes get bombed, and they flee with nothing. If that happened to us here, we wouldn't know what to do."

Ethel agreed. "We are so fortunate that we've never gone through anything like that."

"During the Civil War, it was awful here." Sharon placed a "d" after the word *she*. "Eight points," she informed Mildred, the scorekeeper. "People were left with nothing. Think of Scarlet O'Hara."

It had been years since Ethel had seen *Gone with the Wind*.

"In the end, all she had was a pair of curtains?" Sharon turned the board toward Ethel.

"No, Sharon, you're wrong," Joyce said. "Scarlet was left with curtains more in the middle of the movie than in the end."

Joyce was always good about pointing out when people were wrong.

Following Sharon's turn, the *A* Ethel that had been eyeing was still vacant, so she played her *Z* and *X* for the word "zax." And, the X landed on a double word score tile. "Thirty-eight points."

"What does it mean?" Mildred asked.

"I can't remember." But, she remembered playing the word before.

"We should change the rules. You have to define what it means when you lay it down," Mildred grumbled.

"I don't know why, but I've been eating grapefruit more lately, and my gall bladder hasn't acted up." Sharon graciously changed the subject.

"That's 'cause grapefruit helps you break down fats. But, if you're a diabetic, it can mess up your meds," Mildred said. Her opinion was highly regarded because her daughter was a CNA.

"I hope no one here is a diabetic." Joyce perked up as she peered around the table. "Because I'd like to challenge Ethel to a Sticky Bun Baking Contest, and have you girls be the judges." She smiled brightly.

Please, someone put the woman in her place.

Mildred swallowed.

"What a fun idea." Sharon swallowed, too.

"I've never made sticky buns, so you win." Ethel shrugged.

"Just use the same dough that you used for the fair," Joyce said. Easy for her to say; hers didn't need a warning label. "And follow a sticky bun recipe for the rest."

"I don't know if I can repeat it. You see, I prayed about it, girls." Ethel glanced back and forth between Mildred and Sharon. "I prayed that the Lord would make them providentially delicious and He did. And, I accidentally combined two recipes. God only knows if I'll ever be able to repeat it again. When I wrote out the recipe card for the fair, I had to guess on every ingredient."

Silence followed while she waited for Joyce to bring up the Rhodes affair.

"Just guess again," Mildred added a one shoulder shrug.

"What Thursday should we set our contest for?" Joyce scanned the nearby wall for a calendar.

Ethel shook her head. She couldn't give her girlfriends tummy aches and—

"Ethel, I *love* sticky buns." Sharon pleaded and smacked her lips together like she could already taste the gooey caramel.

"One month." Mildred lifted her squatty purse to her lap and clicked it open. She set a bottle of baby aspirin on the table, followed by a packet of Kleenex, a Sudoku puzzle book, a bottle of Beano, her long, plastic pill box, and lastly, she pulled out her little pocket-sized calendar.

While Mildred thumbed through the pages, Ethel's gaze locked on the small white bottle of Beano. Mildred swore up and down that the little pills worked like magic.

"Four Thursdays from today is October 17th."

Covering her mouth with one hand, Ethel stared at the Beano. Could she possibly pull it off?

"What's the prize? There has to be a prize," Sharon said.

"Let's see, the loser . . ." Joyce said thoughtfully. "Has to disclose their recipe in its entirety to everyone seated here today."

"What about Betty?" Sharon asked.

"I meant Betty, too," Joyce said like she already knew her.

"The loser's recipe? Who wants that?" Sharon crinkled her brow.

"The winner," Joyce said matter of fact.

Ethel's inside churned. Why she ever invited her neighbor to join them today was beyond her. She should have just played with a dummy.

"Let's see . . . the loser has to write the recipe to a T in legible, easy-to-read print on a 4x6 recipe card and give one to each of us. And, dot, dot, dot," Joyce said, poking her finger three times in the air, "we both have to use the SAME dough we used at the fair."

The woman should have been a lawyer.

Sharon turned to stare at Ethel.

Mildred did, too.

She'd already told them that she wouldn't share her prizewinning recipe.

Then she recalled that Joyce had used her coveted dinner roll dough for the cinnamon rolls that she'd entered at the fair. Ethel swallowed. She'd been after the recipe for years. But Joyce never shared.

"I thought you couldn't share." Ethel didn't hide her confusion. "That your dough's a secret-family-recipe that your grandmother on her deathbed made you vow that you'd never share?"

"And, I don't think I'll have to." Joyce smiled, holding her arm stiffly across the table toward Ethel.

"Shake on it," Mildred said.

If for some odd reason Ethel won, she'd win Joyce's dinner roll recipe that for the past six years had earned third place at the fair. And, if for some reason, Ethel lost, she'd have to share—what she'd planned to anyway in this year's Christmas card—the truth behind her prizewinning cinnamon rolls.

While they shook hands, there was a gleam in Joyce's eyes. And, most likely there was one in Ethel's, too.

Chapter Ten

After the Scrabble girls left, Ethel sat at her kitchen table and stared at the recipe card that had accompanied her rolls to the fair. Without the aged whipping cream, she never would have achieved the sourdough taste. And now, due to Joyce's rules, she had to make the dough all over again.

In order to win, she'd have to sour the whipping cream and knowingly give her friends tummy aches and flatulence.

She had to buy Beano.

If she was going to compete, she had to win. And, if for some reason, Ethel won, she'd be like Joyce and never share this recipe. This was one family secret that should remain a secret.

Now, to figure out the sauce. She pulled her cookbooks out of the cupboard to the left of the sink and set them on the table. Then she poured herself a hot cup of coffee, sat down, and began her search.

Wouldn't you know it, out of the six, large cookbooks that she owned, not one had a sticky bun recipe. She dog-eared a Caramel Pecan Frosting recipe that sounded interesting and sighed.

Exhausted from the Scrabble party and all that hosting entailed, she just wanted to try something easy.

In the fridge, there was a store-bought caramel topping for ice cream. What could be easier than that? She poured the contents of the jar into her eight-inch square Pyrex, and it perfectly covered the bottom of the pan. Was she already onto something?

She rinsed the jar at the sink. And, then feeling a tad curious, leaned toward the window, and peered east toward Joyce's place.

The black-eyed Susan plants that Ethel had shared with her over a decade ago brightened this side of her neighbor's white picket fence. A silly riddle popped into her head.

"Why did the aphid cross the road?

"To visit Joyce's black-eyed Susans on the other side."

She giggled at her nonsense.

From a distance, Joyce's flowers looked so pretty, but her house looked like it was frowning. Off and on through the years—usually when they'd squabbled—she'd felt that way about the white, boxy house across the street.

At the counter, Ethel rolled out half a loaf of Rhodes dough that she'd thawed in the microwave. Then she slathered on softened butter, and liberally sprinkled a cinnamon and brown sugar mixture over the top. Next, she followed her usual steps for making cinnamon rolls. Lastly, she nestled pecan halves in the sauce and placed the one-inch slices of dough on top of them.

Oh, phooey! She'd forgotten to toast the pecans! She'd distinctly heard Joyce mention that step. It would have to wait until next time.

Over the next hour, the rolls doubled in size, filling the pie plate like a puffed daisy. Ethel slid them into a preheated 350-degree oven. Eighteen minutes later, the timer dinged. The house smelled heavenly, and the buns were a wonderful golden brown on top. With the help of a cooling rack, Ethel inverted the pan over a large plate.

A sea of runny sauce flooded the sticky buns. Using the flat side of a butter knife, she parted the watery caramel, revealing an unbaked gooey center.

"Phooey!" In a tangled gooey web, the rolls slid back inside the pan. Sauce splashed out the sides and all over the counter to dribble down the face of her white cabinets. She shoved the whole mess back into the oven.

What had she gotten herself into?

After another ten minutes of baking, the tops of the messy rolls were darker than she preferred, but the center finally appeared cooked. Ethel wrote on a nearby sticky note: *The last 10 minutes of baking, tent with foil.* On the second note, she penned: *Toast the pecans!* She stuck the notes to the front of the fridge.

Now she just had to scrub the kitchen from top to bottom and wait for Jimmy, her taste tester, to get home.

Jimmy placed the black rubber plunger in the center of the twelve-by-twelve linoleum tile. Gripping the end of the long, wooden handle, he pushed down, bending his knees until the plunger head deflated to the floor. Then, with solid suction, he lifted up. That tile wasn't loose either. Neither was the next white tile or the next black tile after that. When he reached the end of the row, he glanced back at Vance.

With an elbow on the counter and a pencil behind one ear, his boss appeared to be reading the funnies again. His shoulders were shaking so much.

Three customers were seated in the reception area; quite a few, considering there was only one vehicle in the bay and fifteen minutes left on the clock.

Every other tile, Jimmy glanced over at them to see at least one of them peering over the top of their newspaper or around the side of their magazine at him. Maybe hazing the new employee was something Bill's Tires of Moscow printed in their monthly newsletter and over the years had developed a following. Maybe Jimmy King or James King, as Vance liked to call him, was the featured employee of the month, the rising star at Bill's Tires.

And then again, maybe his imagination was getting the better of him.

In the newsletter, they'd probably featured the picture that Vance had snapped of Jimmy his first day of work when he'd shown up with Fonzie-styled hair. The caption probably read something like: This Thursday, September 19th at 5:30 p.m. enjoy free coffee and watch James King, our new employee, plunge floor tiles. And, remember to bring your newspaper.

When Jimmy reached the steel display of tires, he paused behind it like a curtain and stretched his aching back. *Lord, this is getting old.* In the silence that followed, he listened for reassurance.

"Where are you, Jimmy?" Vance's voice, though loud, was far from his usual bossy tenor.

"Plunging tiles, sir." He centered the plunger in the nearest tile and continued the mind-numbing routine.

"Come 'ere. You missed a whole row."

Heat climbed Jimmy's neck as he strolled toward the counter. This was the exact section he'd checked last night, and he'd been thorough.

"Start right here," Vance tapped the tile beneath his foot, "and head that way." He nodded toward the coffee machine.

"That would be south, sir." Jimmy had always been good at directions, and following them.

"Vance, are we going to paint the windows?" he asked, over his shoulder.

"What do you mean?"

"Well, the Lewiston store has an artist who comes in and paints a big snowman on the window about the first week in October."

"Huh?"

"You know, the bottom snowball looks like a radial tire with chains."

"No, I don't know."

"I always thought he should hold a big sign that says: *Think Snow before you Go*."

"Who should?" Vance frowned.

"The snowman. But they didn't have room for him to hold a sign last year. Their windows aren't as large as ours are."

"What are you going on about?"

"Our windows here are big enough for the snowman to hold the sign." Jimmy waved the plunger toward the expansive front windows.

"We don't need to. See, we're smarter in Moscow than they are in the Valley. Soon as it snows here, people know it's time to get their winter tires. They don't need a snowman to tell them." Vance flicked a hand. "Get back to work."

No snowman in the window? They were missing out. Probably two-thousand cars drove slowly by their windows each day, not that he'd ever counted, and he didn't want to give Vance any ideas.

A customer in the reception area lowered the paper a smidge to eye Jimmy.

Except for the tile plunging and looking like a doofus in front of customers, he liked his job. Working here was worth at least an hour in the gym. The constant routine of moving and lifting tires had built up the muscles in his shoulders, back, and quads. He'd never really had muscles before his job at Bill's. Plus, he was making new friends; and, at six bucks an hour, he earned close to a dollar over minimum wage. But . . . he countered, Bill's Tires of Moscow had hazing the new guy down to a science.

Next week, they'd probably sell tickets.

The little wood bird in the clock in Ethel's living room cuckooed six times. She peered out the window above her kitchen table. Her gaze included the white picket fence that ran the perimeter of her corner lot and Jimmy's shimmery green car as he pulled in front of the detached garage. She poured a large glass of milk and set it on the table.

The back door soon clicked open.

"I need you to wash your hands and sit down," she said.

"Okay, Grandma. Am I late?" His broad-shouldered frame filled the doorway.

"No, honey, I'm just in here dying . . . of curiosity, that's all." Oh, what would she do without Jimmy? They were in this together, just the two of them. Jimmy and her against Joyce. Heaven knew she needed God and an army to beat the woman again.

"Is everything okay?" He soaped up at the sink.

"Yes, and no. Joyce had to sub at my Scrabble party today." She waited until he was seated kitty-corner to her before continuing.

He folded his arms on top of the table.

"In the middle of our game, she challenged me to a Sticky Bun Baking Contest. The girls just ganged up on me. And now, if I don't follow through, I'll look like a coward."

"It's called peer pressure, Grandma."

"I know." She felt her shoulders sink. "I still haven't outgrown it."

"I don't think I have either." He frowned.

She eyed him over the top of her cup. He was lean and fit and could easily afford ten or more extra pounds. "Thank heaven you're here."

"Why do you say that?"

"I'll probably be baking for the next month."

"The next month?"

"Yes. I've never made them before, and they gave me a month to figure them out." She nodded toward the plate of saucy-looking rolls. "I need your honest opinion."

"The day's ending on a better note." Using his bare hand, he separated a roll from the pan. Sauce dripped onto the table before he stuffed half the bun in his mouth, and chewed.

"What do you mean *better* note?" His dark eyes appeared somber. "Is your boss still hazing you?"

His mouth curved down as he nodded. "You know how guys are." The other half of the roll disappeared into his mouth, and with a chipmunk's cheek on one side, he chewed. All of his tire slinging had worked up an appetite.

"I had to plunge tiles this afternoon, this time with an audience." He set an elbow on the table. "I must have looked like the biggest doofus."

No wonder he wasn't his sparkling self.

While he told her about his crummy afternoon, she poured him a second glass of milk and tried to be a good listener.

He reached for his third roll.

"Slow down!" Ethel held out a hand. "You need to tell me what you think? Are they great? How can I improve?" She adjusted her glasses and readied a pen.

"How come you're not trying one?" His gaze narrowed. "Did you use old whipping cream again?"

"No." She giggled. "I'm just watching my waistline." She patted at the stubborn roll the diameter of a hula hoop above her elastic waistband pants. "When you think I'm onto something, I'll sample them. Am I onto something?"

"I'm a guy, Grandma. I'll eat anything."

She tried not to frown. "I know they're edible, but are they good? *Really* good?"

"Well . . . let me see." He transferred another roll to his mouth and chewed thoughtfully. "They're *really* saucy."

"They're supposed to be. They're *sticky buns*."

He paused from chewing and glanced from her to the two remaining rolls. "They are? Hmm... Have you ever been to Ireland's Café in Potlatch?"

"Not for years. And, I've never had one of their sticky buns." But she'd seen them walk by. The rolls had been the size of a dinner plate.

"We used to stop there on our way home from Grandma Lou's. Now, *Ireland's* has great sticky buns."

"What's so great about them?" She readied her pen.

"Well, compared to Ireland's, this sauce," he eyed the bun, "tastes more like a caramel apple like you'd have at the fair. Shouldn't it be more cinnamony and buttery?"

"Probably." *More cinnamony and buttery*. Ethel penned the words. "Go on."

"I'm not saying it's bad." He swished his mouth around, thoughtfully. "But, you wouldn't win *any* contest with these."

He eyed the last two rolls in the pan. "Can I have another one?"

Chapter Eleven

The following Monday, while a pan of sticky buns cooled on the counter, Ethel tried to focus on a crossword puzzle. With baking still on the brain, she was having a difficult time concentrating. She knew if she didn't keep track, the recipes she had and hadn't tried would soon blur into one big muddle. She rose and grabbed a pad of sticky notes and a pen and returned to her old corduroy recliner.

She titled her first note Sticky Buns #1. Then penned: *Rhodes dough, jarred caramel sauce was too runny. Ugh! Didn't toast the pecans.* On the next note, she labeled today's experiment as *Sticky Buns #2: Rhodes dough, toasted the pecans, Caramel Pecan Frosting recipe. Upped the butter to one-quarter cup.*

Today's sauce was a boiled frosting that was supposed to top a cake, but she'd deemed it worth a try. Time would tell.

It smelled good.

The phone rang behind her.

Ethel set her stash on the coffee table and with a kink in her back walked to the curio cabinet to answer it. "Hello," she said into the receiver.

"Ethel, are you busy tonight?"

The voice on the other end sounded like Quinn, but she knew better than to blurt *No, I'm not busy tonight.* What if it was Don? It had been less than a week since he'd called. After only a short greeting, it was hard to tell two deep male voices apart. No wonder Katherine had been so flustered last semester.

"Is this Quinn?" She finally had the intelligence to ask.

"Ye-es, Ethel, it's Quinn."

"No, I'm not busy tonight." Now that Katherine was in Potlatch, Ethel was seeing more of her granddaughter's boyfriend than she'd expected.

"Good. It's a beautiful night, and I was wondering if you'd like to drive up to Paradise Ridge with me to watch the sunset?"

"Aw . . ." Ethel's heart just melted.

"And, there's something very important that I'd like to speak with you about."

She pressed a hand to her mouth, cupping a giggle. He was going to pop the question to Katherine soon. She knew it in her bones. Hopefully, they'd have a long engagement to make up for their short courtship. They hadn't been a real couple all that long. And, Quinn was such a gem, while Katherine was more like a . . . diamond. But rings often matched gems and diamonds together.

"That sounds wonderful."

"Good. Bring a blanket. The temperature drops suddenly this time of year."

"I'll grab a jacket, too." Winter on the Palouse often made its debut in early October.

Ethel shrugged on a coat, grabbed a wool blanket and, in the kitchen, wrote a little note for Jimmy: *Gone with Quinn.* It almost sounded like "Gone with the Wind." She giggled and stuck the yellow sticky note on the front of the white cabinet to the left of the sink.

As soon as Jimmy got home, he'd wash his hands, grab a glass of milk, and probably be on the hunt for the pan of sticky buns for the day. That morning, she'd made the mistake of telling him she was going to bake another batch. Ethel wanted to be present to watch and take notes, get a feel for what went right and wrong with the recipe.

After last Thursday's messy buns, she'd been afraid to flip today's batch. So, the golden-brown rolls remained in the pan, and they looked delicious. She planned to try one tonight after supper.

If she wanted to taste one, she really should write another note for Jimmy. On the second sticky note, she penned: *Don't eat until after dinner. They're my sticky buns. –G.* Now that the rolls were cooled, she covered them with Saran Wrap and stuck the sticky note on top.

As she started for the back door, she recalled her last batch and how Jimmy had finished the entire pan of sticky buns in one sitting, and how he'd averaged only two bites per bun. Maybe it was best not to tempt him. These rolls were important.

She rerouted herself, grabbed the pan off the counter and looking around, stopped in the doorway to the living room. Where could she hide them? The heavenly smell wafting through the house was proof of their existence.

Jimmy wouldn't think to search inside her sewing basket. The pan wouldn't fit unless she took everything out of it, but then where would she hide all that fluff? Without having to relocate things, she could slide the pan under the ruffled hem of the couch, but there were undoubtedly dust bunnies under there.

Quinn's dark blue Volvo rolled past the front windows before taking a right onto her little side street.

Retaining the pan of rolls in her grip, Ethel hurried through the kitchen and pulled the back door closed behind her. Then she took the narrow concrete walkway to the side gate. She'd raised three boys and knew firsthand that telling a hungry, young man not to eat the sticky buns left on the counter was like telling a dog not to scratch.

She closed the picket gate behind her, opened the empty mailbox, and slid the pan of sticky buns inside at a slight slant. The postman always came before one o'clock. They'd be safe here.

And, then she raised the flag to remind herself of their hiding place.

Quinn drove east of town through the rolling hills. The further they got away from Logan Street, the more Ethel felt the stress of the Sticky Buns Contest slip off of her shoulders. It was good to get away from her oven, from her roses, from Joyce her neighbor.

On the right-hand side of the road, the old Slurp and Burp building came into view. In its day, the pool hall had proved quite the social gathering place in their little college town.

"It's been decades since I've been to Paradise Ridge," Ethel admitted, gazing out her side of the car. The freshly plowed fields rolled into patches of distant evergreens.

"Katherine and I've driven up here a couple of times now." Quinn glanced over at her.

"Edwin and I used to make the drive every spring." Most often, winter on the Palouse drug on into the month of May. When the crocuses popped up, and the snow melt revealed nibbles of greenery in the hills, the early months of spring felt like a welcome thaw of the soul.

The roadside changed from open fields to timber. Taking a right, Quinn drove up the gravel mountain roads toward Paradise Ridge. "Farmer's Almanac is predicting a hard winter, so I thought we'd better get in a sunset while we can. My car isn't four-wheel drive."

"That's too bad. And don't forget, you have something *very important* that you wanted to share with me." Through the evergreens, glimpses of the distant rolling hills came into view.

"I won't forget." After they'd climbed the final slope, Quinn parked the car in a grassy area. Like a canvas, the hills in their shades of autumnal glory rolled softly into the horizon. They had the view entirely to themselves.

They sat down on a dark wool quilt in the tall grass. God had painted extra coral and fluorescent pink in tonight's sunset, and she couldn't dismiss the notion that it was just for them.

"How can anyone not believe in God?" Ethel whispered.

"You sound just like Katherine."

She marveled at the peace in his voice. Only a month ago he'd been so frazzled, trying to wait until Katherine finished her masters before he pursued his feelings for her, and having to ward off Doctor Brad in the meantime.

"I'm going to ask your granddaughter to marry me next December."

Tears blurred her vision. In an old-fashioned kind of way, it felt like he was proposing to Katherine now.

"Next December?"

"Yes." He laughed softly.

"Wow!" He was going to wait an entire year. That was good. They'd be a couple longer. He'd get to know Katherine that much better.

Quinn glanced over at her. "The professors' group and I . . . well, we're planning something special. It'll take some ingenuity to pull it off. I want the proposal to be a surprise for Katherine. A complete surprise."

"An entire year of planning? How romantic." She had already proven to Quinn that she could keep a secret.

"The plan's intricate and still in its infancy. I'll share more when I can."

She suppressed a giggle. She couldn't wait.

Sharing the sunset with Quinn had Ethel feeling a tad sentimental during the drive home.

"I made a new batch of sticky buns today," she informed him as they neared her place.

"Sticky buns?" He sounded pleased.

"Yes. I hid them in the mailbox in case Jimmy didn't have enough willpower."

"I saw you slide something in there." Quinn chuckled.

"He ate my last batch—an entire panful— right in front of me. And afterward, he told me… 'those sticky buns couldn't win *any* contest.'"

Quinn had another chuckle. "Well, if you ever need another taste tester, I'm more than happy to help." He took a right off of the Troy Highway onto Logan and then as he turned left at her little side street, his headlights shone briefly on her mailbox.

Were her eyes deceiving her? She turned in her seat as he drove past.

"I could have sworn I left the flag up!"

"You did. I saw you. You don't think Jimmy found them?" Quinn parked behind her Chevy Nova and turned off the engine.

"No. He's never gotten the mail. Why would he start now, when the flag was up?"

Ethel mumbled all the way to the mailbox.

With Quinn by her side, she wrestled the latch free and pulled down the metal lid to peer inside. Except for a few envelopes propped against the side, the box was empty.

"Of all days for the mailman to be late!" she groaned, pulling out the letters.

"You don't think . . ." Quinn's voice trailed off.

"No." Ethel glared at him. "Why in the world would I leave a whole pan of sticky buns for the postman? I've never even met the man. And I left a note on them!"

"What'd it say?" Quinn strode ahead to hold open the gate.

A knot formed in her gut. Setting a hand on top of the picket, she peered up at him. "*Don't eat until after dinner. They're my sticky buns*–and then I wrote a Capital G followed by a period. I was hurrying and didn't want to spell out *Grandma*.

"Oh, pooh!" She frowned. "With my luck, they're probably the best batch I'll ever bake."

Chapter Twelve

Ethel stirred non-dairy creamer into her morning cup of coffee. And, then curious about her grandson's little routine, she shook the can of Reddi-Wip and piped the whipping cream around and around the surface of her coffee.

With her elbows on the table, she closed her eyes and took her first sip. Not bad. Not bad, at all. She couldn't name a dessert that didn't benefit from a dollop of whipped cream. Not that coffee was a dessert; but, when you added whipped cream, it was.

She reached for her Bible in the center of the table and opened to Galatians. When she was only halfway through chapter two, her head ached. There was so much going on in the first paragraph. Then she remembered to pray and ask the Lord to give her discernment. "Help me. This is a tough chapter."

While she continued reading, the picture of Jimmy plunging floor tiles bee-bopped into her head. She said a brief prayer for him, sighed and then continued reading. *I have been crucified with Christ and I no longer live, but Christ lives in me. The life I now live in the body, I live by faith in the Son of God, who loved me and gave Himself up for me.*

She'd hit the mother lode.

"Thank you, Lord," she whispered.

Be with Jimmy and his boss. Help him to live by faith. Not by the flesh. Mid-prayer, she heard her grandson wander into the kitchen behind her. His hair was tousled, and he was still in his flannel jammy pants. While he shook cereal into a bowl, Ethel refilled her cup of coffee and poured one for him, too.

"You okay?" she murmured. When a young man looked this groggy in the morning, she knew to keep her voice to a whisper. She'd learned that from Tim.

"I stayed up late, studying. Between my math and literature classes, I have a ton of homework." He set the jug of milk on the table and sat down in the chair to her right.

"Which one comes easier for you?"

"Definitely English. I'm only so-so at math."

She recalled his *Baby, Don't Brake Me* paper upstairs and could only imagine his math scores.

"How's work been? Is your boss still hazing you?"

With his elbows on the table, Jimmy shrugged. "Every evening at 5:30, he's still having me do the Tile Check."

"With the plunger?"

He nodded. "Matt, one of my buddies, thinks he wants me to quit. He said he's never seen Vance haze someone for so long."

"If you walked to school, honey, you wouldn't even need a job."

"I love my car." The wide-eyed look he flashed her told her he was no longer half asleep. "And, I like working at Bill's Tires. Vance could haze me for a year. I won't quit."

Call it Pettigrew pride or stamina, but she had just seen it surface.

"I've been praying for you."

"Thanks, Grandma." His chest expanded before he took a sip of coffee.

Who did this Vance fellow think he was? And why was he hazing her grandson?

"Honey, do you think anyone would notice if I sat in the reception area at your work some afternoon before closing?"

"Grandma . . ." Brows furrowed, he shook his head. "Only customers sit in the reception area."

"What if I was a customer?"

"Your last name's King. They'd know." Jimmy poured milk over his bowl of Fiber One, and squirted a wavy pile of Reddi-Wip on top.

"I could go by Pettigrew, my maiden name."

"Your tires are fine." He locked eyes with her.

"If I wanted to see you in action, what would be the best time for me to show up?"

"What are you going to do? Puncture a tire?"

"I don't know."

He rocked his chair away from the table. His cereal was going to get soggy if he wasn't careful. "You'd have to pay in cash. They'd see Ethel King on your check and..." He shook his head. "Don't do it. The guys saw you the other day, and they know my grandmother has a '72 red Chevy Nova."

"I was wearing my hat."

"And you had your black purse."

"I have other purses and clothes." She even had another vehicle—Edwin's old truck sat idle in their detached garage.

"Don't do it, Grandma. I'd hear about it for the rest of my life."

She toyed with her lower lip. If she went, she'd bring her Polaroid camera and take pictures. If she did witness the hazing, she'd want proof in case Jimmy ever needed it. If she was going to go, she should go soon. The boss probably wouldn't have him plunging tiles forever.

Ethel knew if she went to Bill's Tires alone, she'd feel conspicuous. Who could she get to go with her?

She called her sister Gladys first. Gladys declined because she was having her neighbors for dinner. It didn't sound quite right, but that's what she'd said.

Joyce came to mind. Ethel quickly negated that idea. Tonight, she needed someone who'd be on her side. Joyce was rarely on her side. Mildred came to mind. No, she wouldn't invite her. Mildred would think she was a fruitcake. Betty still had her daughter and son-in-law in town. She dialed Sharon next.

Sharon might be terrible at Scrabble, but when you needed someone to be on your side, there wasn't a dearer person in the entire world.

"Sharon, it's Ethel. Are you busy tonight between five and six o'clock?"

"No, Ethel. Why?"

"It's a long story, but I need you to wear a dress. I'm going to wear one, too. We're going to look like two little, old ladies out on the town."

"Oh, Ethel, I haven't been out on the town for years." Sharon giggled. "Do you know at my last doctor appointment that the nurse practitioner couldn't even find a pulse?"

"Well . . . before you get too excited, we're just going to Bill's Tires to sit in their reception area so I can take pictures. I want evidence of Jimmy's boss hazing him."

"Oh! It sounds like a mystery." Sharon loved reading mysteries.

"It is. Why would a grown man in his right mind have Jimmy plunge floor tiles?"

"Huh?"

"You'll see. Thank you, Sharon. You're a dear, dear friend."

"Awh, Eth—"

Ethel hung up the phone. Why, if Sharon were here in person, she'd give her a big ole hug.

"Lord, forgive me for all the times I didn't want to be her Scrabble partner. I have to get over this having to win all the time. It's become a disease."

Ethel returned to the kitchen, took a loaf of Rhodes dough out of the freezer and set it on the counter to thaw, and then she sat down at the table to scour more cookbooks.

Chapter Thirteen

Since Jimmy had told her not to wear a hat to Bill's Tires, Ethel fussed a little more than usual with her hair. Not that anyone at Bill's would notice, but the pink floral motif on her dress also had a touch of blue that matched perfectly with her light-blue purse and pumps.

Sharon arrived at five o'clock, wearing a white cardigan over her royal blue polyester dress, the one with the large hibiscus flowers on it.

"We look like spring and summer in the fall," Sharon said, joining Ethel in the kitchen.

"You're right about that. After we get home from Bill's, you can sample today's experiment." Ethel pointed to the eight-inch square pan of sticky buns on the table.

"I dunno. I'd hate to disqualify myself as a judge. I like Joyce, don't get me wrong, but I've never seen anyone make up rules as fast as she can."

"She has a lot of rules." There was something she needed to do... What was it? "Oh, I almost forgot, I need to call Les Schwab." Ethel started for the living room.

"I thought we're going to Bill's Tires?"

"We are. But I can't call Bill's with the question that I have. They'll know it's me."

"Whatever you say."

After finding Les Schwab Tires in the Latah County directory, Ethel dialed their number.

Sharon stood nearby, monkeying in her purse.

"Good afternoon. This is Les Schwab, Kevin speaking. How may I help you?"

"Yes, young man, I have a question," Ethel cleared her unusually dry throat.

"Yes. How may I help you?"

"If I showed up at your shop with, say . . . a nail in my tire, well, is that a pretty common . . . ailment?"

In the silence that followed, Sharon nudged by her to the mirror above the curio cabinet, where she dabbed on hibiscus-colored lipstick. She'd only recently stopped coloring her hair black, and her natural gray was a vast improvement, it brought out the pink in her cheeks.

"Are you still there, Les Schwab?" Ethel asked into the ensuing silence.

"Yes. Are you able to drive it here, ma'am? There's about a thirty-five-minute wait at the moment."

Why wouldn't she be able to drive it there? Did he think she sounded too old to drive?

"While I have you on the phone, Kenneth, what are some other believable things that can happen to a tire? Things you might see on a daily basis?"

"I'm sorry, ma'am. Didn't you say your tire's leaking?"

"Not at the moment. That's the trouble."

"What was that . . . ma'am?" He chuckled.

She always liked when men called her *ma'am*. Well, younger men, that is.

"Most often people come to us because their tires are already having uh… ailments."

"What is something *easy* I can do to my tire so I can come see you guys? I'm seventy-one years old, and a widow."

Sharon gawked at her.

Ethel pressed her index finger to her lips, shushing her.

"Well . . ." There was an echo to his voice now like maybe he'd hit the speaker button by accident, or perhaps on purpose. "In answer to your question, ma'am, a common way to damage your tires would be to drive around a construction site. This happens quite a bit. People don't know they have a nail in their tire, and it's in there causing a slow leak. Then all of a sudden their tire's flat."

"Well, what if I just took a hammer and a nail to my tire instead?" Hand on hip, Ethel waited through a muffled silence on the other end of the line.

"Have you ever tried to hammer a nail into four-ply rubber, ma'am? We don't recommend it." There was a clicking sound; then his voice no longer projected the echo. "Our business is steady. It's more like a forty-five-minute wait here at the moment. We don't need you to damage your tires on our account. Though we do appreciate your, uh... loyalty."

They were so nice at Les Schwab. She wished Jimmy worked there.

"Should I use a construction-type nail and hammer then, Ken? Is that what you're saying?" There were some long nails in the garage and a heavy-duty hammer that had a meat-tenderizing face.

"Those do the most damage, ma'am."

"Thank you, Kenny, you've been most helpful."

"Thank you, ma'am. We look forward to your business."

Ethel was the first to hang up.

"He was such a nice, young man," she told Sharon. "But . . . at one point it almost sounded like he put us on speaker phone."

"Oh, Ethel, he probably did. Your voice was probably blasted over the intercom like a bluelight special." When Sharon used to work at the old K-mart in Moscow, her favorite part of the job had been intercomming the bluelight special and watching from her second-floor office as people stampeded through the aisles like water buffalo.

They grabbed their purses and hustled out the back door and along the narrow concrete walkway to the detached garage. While the overhead lights flickered and buzzed, Ethel walked to the driver's side of Edwin's old seafoam green Ford. What in the world could she pretend was wrong with a truck that had only been driven twice in the past decade?

"How are the tires on your car, Sharon?"

"I wished you'd asked last week. My son-in-law just had my car serviced for the winter."

"That was nice of him." Ethel pulled open a long, shallow drawer in the Craftsman rollaway. "I can't take my Nova. I delivered lunch one day to Jimmy when he was at work, and now he's afraid they'll recognize me."

"What can I do to help?" Sharon asked.

"Here, hold this nail." Ethel handed her a long, four-inch construction-type nail. Then she continued pulling open drawers in the rollaway in her search for a hammer.

"Here, I'll put our purses in the cab." Sharon picked Ethel's purse off the dusty workbench.

In one of the middle drawers, Ethel found the heavy hammer with the meat tenderizing head.

"Well, I do declare, our worries have been solved." Sharon's voice echoed from the other side of the garage.

"What do you mean?"

"Your tire over here is pert-near flat."

"What?' She couldn't believe their luck. She had to see it to believe it. With the hammer in her grip, she followed Sharon's voice around to the passenger-side and almost walked straight into the side mirror. Sure enough, the tire was half spent.

"How can a tire go flat just sitting in here?" Ethel marveled. It was an answer to a prayer unspoken.

"Good thing Bill's Tires is close." Sharon clicked the seatbelt around her middle.

"I just can't get over it. The truck's only been driven two times in the last ten years. This summer, Katherine drove it to Potlatch, the day she went to the creek and stepped on a wine bottle, and then Quinn drove it home the next day." Ethel adjusted the mirrors.

"That's right. You told me about that terrible mess."

"There's a purpose to everything." Ethel backed out of the garage and onto the gravel side street. Because of Katherine's injury, Quinn had determined the depths of his feelings for her. And of course, Doctor Brad's obvious interest in his patient also helped to speed things along.

"Oh, Ethel, this old truck is like taking a trip down memory lane."

"For me, too. This truck was Edwin's pride and joy."

She turned right onto the Troy Highway, and the transition from gravel to the smooth highway made the steering wheel pull even harder to the right.

"I've heard before that if you drive with a flat tire too far, you can damage the hubcap," Sharon said.

"Not the hubcap. You mean the rim." If Edwin knew she was driving his truck with a flat tire, he'd turn over in his grave.

"Oh, what do I know?" Sharon waved a hand. "All I know is it's a good thing we were planning to go to Bill's Tires."

The two-lane highway was busy with dinner hour traffic. Ethel locked her elbows at her sides and gripped the steering wheel tightly with both hands.

"Oh, Ethel." Sharon held onto the strap above the window like it was a lifeline.

"I love how you changed the Bible study," Ethel said, trying to get her mind off their dire situation. "I'm getting more out of it, only reading one chapter a day."

"Maybe it's because we're getting old, but I feel the same way." Sharon clicked open her handbag and pulled out her little purse-sized Bible. "This morning's chapter was powerful."

At the intersection of the Lewiston Highway, Ethel rolled the truck to a stop. Bill's Tires large white building sat a block off to their right. A beacon to the downtown area.

"Here it is . . ." Sharon ran a finger down the page. "I have been crucified with Christ and I no longer live, but Christ lives in me."

The light turned green. *Please, get us there. Driving on a rim is really, really bad.* Ethel steered the crippled truck north and then lurched into Bill's front parking lot. When she turned off the engine, a hissing sound emanated from Sharon's side of the vehicle.

Hallelujah! There was still air to spare.

She relaxed back into the seat.

"The life I now live in the body, I live by faith in the Son of God who loved me and gave Himself for me." Sharon held the little book against her chest. "Oh, Ethel, how can we take a love like this lightly?"

"We can't." Ethel felt convicted, too. The grandmother in her just wanted to pounce on this Vance fellow. Let him know who was king. But, as Sharon had just reminded her, she had to die to self. Die to pride.

"Something's going on with Jimmy's boss. He keeps picking on my sweet grandson. You'll see. That's why we're here. We need proof. That's why I brought my camera." Ethel patted her large purse. "If the harassing continues, I'm going to send pictures to the owner."

"Bill Hicks?"

Ethel nodded and glanced over at Sharon. Her friend appeared shorter than usual, probably due to the flat tire on her side of the vehicle.

"Oh, Ethel, I haven't had this much adventure in years." Sharon gripped the handles of her purse in her lap.

"Supposedly, the boss only hazes the new employee for a couple of days. But, in Jimmy's case, it's already been almost two weeks."

Sharon's mouth pinched tight. "Let's say a prayer."

Ethel agreed. "Pray that we get a shot of Jimmy plunging tiles and the boss in the same picture, so we have proof."

"And, we'll pray that he stops hazing Jimmy."

"Yes, but let's get a great picture first," Ethel said because she was a firm believer in the power of prayer.

At the front counter, a beefy young man wrote down Ethel's information while Sharon took a seat behind her in the reception area. There was a low black coffee table with magazines, about a dozen chairs in an L-shape configuration, a short coffee counter, but no trolley popcorn machine.

"Did we miss the popcorn?" Ethel asked.

"We don't have popcorn at Bill's."

"Why, not?" She'd been craving popcorn all day, knowing she was going to be here.

"Because Les Schwab has popcorn."

"Huh?" His dumb response surprised her. What kind of outfit was Jimmy working for anyway? She strolled to the reception area and sat down in the chair on Sharon's left where she had an open view of the front counter.

Hopefully, Vance was working today.

A middle-aged man with *Happy Days*-style hair strolled to the front counter and tapped a tile with the toe of his steel-toed boot. "James King, start over here. You missed this row last night."

Ethel nudged Sharon and whispered, "What's that guy on *Happy Days* called? You know, with the ducktail?"

"Fonzie?"

"Yes! I think Fonzie is Jimmy's boss."

"Oo-oh, I always liked the Fonz."

Jimmy strode into view, carrying a long-handled commercial-grade plunger. He appeared unusually stoic, and a deep flush was evident in his profile. Was he mad about Granddad's truck being up on the lift? Was he mad at her? Even though he was only about fifteen feet away, he didn't glance their direction once.

Like the good employee that he was, Jimmy started on tile number one. Centering the plunger in the square tile, he bent his knees and pushed down until the rubber head was deflated and then he lifted up, checking the suction.

It was something you almost had to see to believe.

"What's he doing, Ethel?"

Tile plunging was just as he'd described: Demeaning. Humiliating. Humbling. Why didn't the boss like him? Ethel pulled a Kleenex out of her purse and held it in front of her nose like a curtain to talk behind. "Jimmy thinks his boss wants him to quit."

"Why doesn't he just fire him?"

"'Cause he hasn't done anything wrong."

"Well, then . . ." Sharon's chest expanded, "Fonzie should be fired."

She'd known Sharon would be on her side.

"I need you to stand up and let me take a picture of you, over by the counter." Ethel jabbed her thumb to her left. "So, I can get Jimmy and his boss in the same shot. Pretend I'm taking your picture."

"I thought you were taking my picture?" Sharon, who didn't have a vain bone in her body, had always loved having her picture taken.

In her royal blue muumuu with the swirling hibiscus and her white cardigan pushed up at the sleeves, Sharon clasped her hands in front of her and smiled like she was standing beside a Princess Cruise ship instead of a tire counter. Ethel held her old Polaroid steady and pressed the button.

Sharon returned to sit in the padded chair beside her. Shoulder to shoulder, they waited for the magic to happen.

Oh pooh! Half the evidence was missing. Only Sharon and the manager had been captured. At the last second, Jimmy must have moved to the next tile.

"Can I keep it?" Sharon whispered.

"Later." Ethel set the picture in her lap.

"Go stand by the coffee counter." This time, Ethel had to focus more on Jimmy.

For this shot, Sharon held her purse in front of her, smiling. Ethel glanced over at Vance, who was now on the phone. Ethel held up the camera, paying more attention to her grandson this time before pushing down the button.

Cheeks flushed with excitement, Sharon hurried over and sat down beside her.

"I love this one." Sharon picked up the first photo and turned it around for the other patron seated near the coffee counter to see.

The scruffy, unshaven man nodded, stifling a yawn.

"You can have it, Sharon. It's yours." Ethel held the latest photo closer against her, so the afternoon light streaming through the windows didn't ruin its development.

It was a nice candid shot of Jimmy in action, but she'd only captured the boss's elbow. "Phooey!"

"Go stand where you did the first time, but closer to . . . Fonzie," Ethel whispered. She needed to hurry and take another picture while Jimmy was in the same vicinity as his boss.

Standing slightly left of Jimmy's boss, with her nose tilted in the air, Sharon wore the exuberant look of an elderly woman on holiday.

Closing her left eye, Ethel peered with her right through the itty-bitty flea-sized hole. She had the manager in the left of the frame. *Please, Lord, please, Lord.* Camera steady, she waited for Jimmy to step into view.

Sharon was now humming something slightly familiar.

The boss's gaze lifted from whatever he was reading and shifted her direction.

Sharon's little tune was so catchy that Ethel had to fight wiggling in her chair. The plunger and Jimmy's arms were in the frame. *One more tile, Jimmy. One more tile.* Now, his whole body was in view, and the boss was looking right at Ethel. Click. She pressed down firmly, holding the camera steady.

"Let me see. Let me see." Sharon hurried over to sit down.

They had the Fonzie guy's attention now.

Ethel slid the developing evidence inside her purse and handed Sharon the second picture—the one of her standing beside the coffee counter.

Sharon studied it, humming and wiggling her shoulders.

Ethel's memory finally retrieved the lyrics. *One, two . . . three o'clock* . . . Rock Around the Clock! Sharon's humming was the hit song from *Happy Days.*

Jimmy's boss rounded the side of the counter and started their direction.

Was he going to confiscate their pictures?

"Stop humming." She ribbed Sharon.

"What you girls got there?" Vance stopped two feet away.

Ethel peered up at him.

"Pictures. Wanna see?" Sharon held up the one of her and Vance together.

"Oh, that's a great one." Holding the corner of the picture, he ran a hand through his salt-and-pepper hair, admiring himself. "Any others?"

"Just this one." Sharon held up the one of her standing by the coffee machine with Jimmy plunging floor tiles in the background and Vance's elbow in the far left. "Oh, what's this fella doing?" Pointing at the photo, Sharon pretended to notice for the first time.

"Checking for loose tiles, ma'am. It's an advanced technique to keep our showroom floor looking its best." He smiled and locked eyes with Ethel. "Wasn't there another photo?"

"What?" Sharon blinked up at him.

In her lap, Ethel gripped the handles of her purse in one hand and, heart thumping, set her other hand on top.

"I thought she took three." He nodded toward Ethel.

"One" Sharon held up a photo in her left. "Two." And the other photo in her right.

"I see." His gaze lowered to Ethel's blue faux leather bag and stayed there.

With both hands gripping the handles, Ethel locked her elbows against her sides. If he so much as—

"Vance . . . do you want me to get that?" Jimmy yelled.

"Huh? No, I'll get it." The man's gaze darted to Ethel, then he turned on his heel and jogged toward the counter.

She hadn't even heard the phone ring.

"Oh, Ethel, feel my pulse." Sharon held out her wrist. "It's just a thumpity, thumpity, thumping."

Ethel pressed two fingers on a nearby vein. "It sure is."

Why, if the phone hadn't rung, she might have thumped Jimmy's boss over the head with her purse. Thank heaven it hadn't come to that. It might have hurt the picture that she was going to send to Bill Hicks tomorrow morning.

Chapter Fourteen

At closing time, the guys were still talking about the goofy grandmas. In the employees' lounge, Jimmy punched out his time card. His knotted stomach felt like he'd eaten an entire pan of Grandma's cinnamon blasts. Thankfully, none of the guys had recognized her as the lunch-toting granny.

"Did you see the old lady's F100?" Matt asked on their way out the double doors.

"Yeah. It was sweet." Jimmy added a chuckle. Sweet was an understatement. Beneath a decade of dust, Grandpa's pride of ownership still shone in the thirty-year-old vehicle.

"It even had the stock V8 engine in it and the old Ford emblem on the hood. I told her if she ever wanted to sell it, to give me a call. Except for the tires, it's in mint condition."

"What'd she say?" Jimmy's heart stretched uncomfortably.

"Awh . . . she didn't want to. But, I gave her my number." Matt waved and made a beeline for his Datsun pickup.

"Yep, see ya tomorrow." Jimmy unlocked his car and slid behind the wheel.

Today, he needed more than a two-minute drive home to unwind. Instead of the Troy Highway, he took the side streets and drove slow. He couldn't believe the stunt Grandma had pulled. He'd only worked at the Moscow location two weeks, and she'd already visited twice. Somehow, he had to nip it in the bud before he was permanently labeled a granny's boy.

When he reached home, there was no extra vehicle parked in back. Either the two were still out and about, or Mrs. Purtell had already left. Curious, Jimmy opened the garage door and flicked on the overhead lights. Grandpa's '65 Ford F100 was parked in the same exact spot, except it now sported a new all-weather Michelin tire.

They'd got all dolled up just to go to Bill's Tires.

How had Tim worded it? *After living with Grandma Ethel, you'll have stories to tell.* He'd only been here two weeks, and he had a humdinger.

He walked up the back steps and clicked the door closed behind him.

"Wash up. Today's the best batch yet." Grandma, in her usual everyday attire—a T-shirt and elastic waistband pants—stood near the table pouring a glass of milk.

While he washed his hands, the window above the sink reflected the scene behind him. Grandma now seated at the table, working a crossword puzzle, pretended nothing out of the ordinary had just happened. Did she think he didn't have a brain? No more than thirty minutes ago, she and Mrs. Purtell had been acting like goofballs at his workplace.

He wasn't going to let her off the hook so easily.

He tossed a towel onto the counter and turned to face her.

"I wish you hadn't gone, Grandma."

"No one will ever know, honey." Her posture stiffened slightly.

He inhaled deeply, hoping she was right.

"Where are the pictures?"

"Right there." Without turning her head, she pointed to the fridge. "Your boss really liked the one of him."

She'd snapped one of Vance. Great! If he ever found out whose Grandma she was, Jimmy might be plunging tiles for the rest of his days. Maybe he should have stayed in

Lewiston. The forty-five-minute drive home would have given him time to unwind, and he could have kept Mike Gregerson for a boss. Compared to Vance, Mike had been a dream.

Hands on hips, he paused in front of the old Frigidaire. Grandma's style of scrapbooking was sticky notes and clunky magnets securing photos to the top half. Near the middle of the collage, he located a snapshot of Mrs. Purtell. Wearing her muumuu and a look of la-la, she stood near the service counter. On the right side of the photo, Vance cradled the phone to his ear while he stapled something. Probably his favorite comics.

"I know you took more than one."

"Did you see the one of me?"

"No." On the right side near the top, he'd missed the photo, the first time around. In the back-gravel driveway, Grandma in her Sunday best, stood holding her purse in front of her near the driver's side door of Grandpa's truck.

The picture pert near melted his heart.

"I realized tonight, how much I love that old truck. I only wish I'd got a picture of Edwin with it. As soon as we got home, I had Sharon take one of me."

"It's a great picture, Grandma." He sat down at the table and taking a swig of milk, knew his moxie was melting.

"Where's the other photos from Bill's?" He lowered the glass.

"There's one of you and Sharon that I already gave her. You wouldn't have liked it, but she did."

"That's not all you took?" Mrs. Purtell had posed for at least three.

Grandma's gaze lifted to the short white curtains with embroidered strawberries. "We would have taken more, but then your boss came over. I'm not very impressed with him." She shimmied her posture a little taller. "I wished you would have told me that Bill's doesn't have popcorn. I thought all tire places had popcorn. By the time I got there, I was just craving it. Sharon was too. We were both so disappointed. But, don't worry, honey. As long as you're working at Bill's, that's the only place I'm buying my tires."

He rubbed his temple, frowning. What had he been about to ask her? It was like Grandma had become an expert in bait and switch.

"How'd you get the tire flat?" He eyed her.

"We didn't have to do a thing. Did you know that rubber gets old and brittle just sitting?" Of course, he knew; he worked in a tire shop. "A stocky young fellow, oh, what was his name . . .? Matt!" She bobbed a finger into the air. "He said it's probably from the sunlight streaming through the garage windows. Did he tell you that he wanted me to replace *all* four tires?"

"No. Remember, he doesn't know we're related?"

"That's right. I didn't have enough cash anyway. And why would I want four new ones? In the last ten years, the only place I've driven the truck is to Bill's Tires."

She had a point.

Closing his eyes, he inhaled deeply.

Love thy Grandma, the soft voice inside his soul whispered.

His eyes warmed. *I love her very much, but right now she's making a mess of—*

"Don't they look beautiful?" Grandma slid a pan of sticky buns right beneath his nose.

He blinked.

"They sure do. What's special about today's batch?" While he eyed the glossy rolls, he reached for her hand and briefly squeezed it.

"I found a recipe for sticky buns on the back of the Karo syrup bottle." She giggled. "Here, I've been scouring all my cookbooks, and I should have been reading bottles."

Jimmy used his fork. After several attempts, he was able to pry one from the pan.

"I baked them right after lunch. Do you want me to heat it up?"

"No, that's all right."

"I've never been a big fan of corn syrup." Grandma readied her pen and paper. "I accidentally added too much once to a batch of caramel corn that I was making, and the boys nicknamed it rock corn. Have you heard that story?"

"No." He took his first bite and paused mid-chew. The rolls didn't look burnt, but something tasted smoky.

"Did you add molasses?"

"Only a tablespoon. The recipe didn't call for it, but I've always loved molasses."

"Whoa!" Leaning back in his chair, he tried not to breathe. "It's like a brick wall of molasses."

"That bad?"

Eyes pinched tight, he nodded. "I usually like molasses." He lowered the bun to his plate and didn't know if he had it in him to take another bite.

"Huh?" Grandma rolled her wrist. "I thought you could eat anything?"

He wasn't a picky eater, but stuff didn't usually taste like charred campfire wood with a hint of cinnamon. He downed the rest of his milk. "Sorry, Grandma."

"We'll just throw them away, then." She rose from the table and opened the cabinet beneath the sink. Holding the pan over the garbage, she gave the bottom a few thumps. "I've never been a big fan of corn syrup. During the war years, sugar was rationed, so my mother used corn syrup to sweeten everything."

"What war was that, Grandma?"

She peered over her shoulder at him, brows narrowed and jaw slack. "World War II. After Pearl Harbor." After grabbing a fork, she pried the buns loose and tossed them into the trash.

"Sorry, Grandma, that's a lot of work to just throw away."

"Not really. I didn't make them from scratch. I cheated with Rhodes."

He nodded and gathered gumption.

"Grandma, I love you. And this is hard to tell you," he raised his voice, while her back was to him, and she ran tap water into the pan, "but please don't go to Bill's Tires again. I'm worried about my job, and my boss, and being labeled *Grandma's Boy*."

She turned off the water, nodding. "I love you, too, honey. I promise." In the reflection of the window above the sink, she met his gaze. "I promise I won't go again; that is, unless you leave your lunch or really, really needed me to . . . for some reason."

It was important to feel needed. He couldn't take that away from her.

Love thy grandma; the voice was softer now. *Love thy grandma.*

Thursday morning after Jimmy left for work, Ethel sat down at her maple table in the living room. And, with a view of the mailbox, she penned her letter to Bill Hicks.

Dear Bill,

My grandson Jimmy King has recently been transferred from your Lewiston store to your Moscow location. Ever since his transfer, Vance, his new boss, has been "hazing" him. Making him do what Jimmy calls the "tile plunge" every evening for about a half hour before closing.

My truck recently had a flat tire, and when I took it in, I was able to get a photo of the hazing. (See enclosed picture.) The woman in the blue dress is my girlfriend Sharon being silly.

Jimmy loves working for your company. He doesn't know about this particular picture or that I'm sending it to you. But, as his grandmother, I couldn't just sit back and do nothing. Not when the good Lord gave me a Polaroid camera.

Sincerely,

Ethel King

She sealed the envelope. Then she called the tire company's corporate office in Spokane and asked for the best address to reach Bill Hicks. With her letter in hand, she took the side gate to her mailbox, put the flag up, and said a prayer.

Betty couldn't come again for Thursday's Scrabble game on account of a dental appointment, and Joyce was ready at the whistle. She even brought over a plate of her famous Parkerhouse Rolls. This month, she was even baking other things besides sticky buns. Ethel couldn't imagine.

Joyce and Ethel were again partners. When the letter bag was only half-empty, they were already in the lead by forty-eight points.

"Talking about our FDA," Sharon said, placing an *E* on the board below a B. Ethel didn't remember anyone talking about the FDA, but that's how Sharon had prefaced it. "What's a cancer doctor called? Starts with an O."

"Oncologist," Ethel said.

"Yes. If an oncologist got cancer, you know what they'd do? They'd go to Mexico or some other country to get cured."

"Everything's driven by money, greed, and . . ." Mildred paused for a moment waiting for Sharon to tell her score.

"Cars?" Sharon said.

Everyone laughed.

Then, Sharon held up four fingers before turning the board for Ethel's play.

Ethel had all the letters for the word "pizza," except for the second *Z* because Scrabble only had one *Z* per board game, which she now deemed a mistake on Milton Bradley's part. Having two *Z*s in her possession would have been stellar. There was an open *U*. *Oh, my*, Ethel couldn't believe her luck and spelled "Putz."

"What does it mean?" Mildred mumbled under her breath.

"I don't remember, but I've heard it before."

"So have I, but I still think you should have to know what it means to play it," Mildred said.

"Putz . . ." Joyce adjusted her wire-framed glasses. "You're such a putz."

"Yes, but what does it mean?" Mildred repeated.

"You know . . ." Sharon's shoulders gave a little swish. "Don't putz around."

The doorbell dinged.

Ethel and Joyce locked eyes. Her neighbor knew as well as she did that the only people who used her front porch were lovebirds or solicitors, and the lovebirds didn't ring the doorbell.

Don't be Don Gardner.

"Ethel, your doorbell dinged," Mildred droned.

Ethel swiveled in her chair and, setting a hand on the table, rose and putzed across the room. Joyce, her usual nosy self, accompanied her halfway. "Nope, it's not the *nice* car I was telling you girls about."

Whose car had she been telling them about? She'd never heard of a gold Buick station wagon described as a *nice* car. Maybe she was thinking of Quinn's Volvo?

Ethel opened the door about a foot wide and then poked her head around.

A mailman wearing a post office blue button-up shirt and knee-length shorts stood on the other side of the screen. Wispy, silver curls ebbed beneath his dark brimmed cap.

"Ethel, Ethel King . . .?" It was like they'd been pen pals for years and were finally meeting. He grinned, holding her square Pyrex pan against him. "Those sticky buns—"

Not wanting Joyce to hear the ensuing conversation, she joined him on the porch, pulling the door closed behind her.

". . . were delicious. Nowadays, folks rarely leave their mailman treats, not like the old days. Now in the old days, we'd get a fruitcake at Christmas, and little treats throughout the years just like clockwork."

She didn't have the heart to tell him that it had all been a thoughtless mistake.

"By the way, I'm Stan." He tipped his hat. Tan and lean, Stan was weathered, too, like he'd trekked the route for forty years before he'd thought to wear a hat.

"I'm Ethel," she said, even though he already knew her name. She glanced toward the window and half expected all three of her friends to be huddled there, wearing her lace curtain panels like a bride's veil.

No one was. But, that didn't mean they weren't looking through the peephole.

"Do you ever make maple bars?"

"No, I haven't."

"Aww . . . those are my favorite." He swallowed.

Ethel's brain finally kicked in. "What'd you think of the sticky buns . . . Stan?"

"They were delicious." He rocked back in his sturdy walking shoes and made an eye roll. "Some of the best I've ever tasted."

That's what she'd been afraid of.

"I obeyed the note and didn't eat them until after dinner. But you were wrong." He grinned. "I could have eaten them during my route. They weren't all that sticky."

"Not all that sticky?" She repeated his sentiments and tried to remember what all had been in the cinnamon pecan frosting experiment.

"Yep. I could easily have eaten them and delivered the mail." He handed her the pan. "Thanks again, Ethel." He started down the steps.

She returned inside and closed the door.

"Who was that?" Mildred asked, without lifting her gaze from the board.

"Just the postman." Ethel strolled through the living room toward the kitchen. After she set the glass pan on the counter, she wrote *More sticky*, on a sticky note and stuck it to the front of the fridge before returning to her seat.

"The postman?" Joyce's brows knit tightly.

"Yes. I don't know how many years he's been delivering our mail, but his name's Stan."

"About eight, and he doesn't bring Pyrex to my door."

"It was a mistake. And, it's a long story."

"Go on . . ." Mildred rolled her hand, no change in her dull expression.

"Well . . ." Ethel glanced across the table at Joyce. "I hid a pan of my baked goodies in our mailbox one evening when Katherine's boyfriend took me to Paradise Ridge to watch the sunset." She was tired of keeping so many secrets. "And, I have to tell you girls, it was even more beautiful than I remember."

"You make my life feel dull." Mildred's shoulders slumped.

"What I don't understand, Ethel," Sharon said, "is, why did you hide your baked goodies in the mailbox in the first place?"

"I was afraid Jimmy would eat them." Joyce's dark penciled brows furrowed even deeper. "It was well after four in the afternoon, and I felt certain that the postman had already been here. He always comes before one."

"Not *always*." Joyce set an elbow on the table.

"Well, usually always. Anyway, while Quinn and I were away, Stan, the mailman, thought the baked goods in the mailbox were for him." Ethel giggled, studying the board. "Now he thinks I'm his new best friend."

"One of my girlfriends, Jackie O . . . sen," Sharon reached inside the letter bag, "her mailman fell in love with her, and she was already married. But Jackie was only in her early twenties at the time."

"And . . . is there a point to this story?" Mildred lifted a Parkerhouse roll off her plate and glanced at Joyce. "By the way, these are delicious."

Joyce smiled.

"Well . . . anyways . . ." Sharon continued, "Jackie used some of those bottled paints that come in car model kits. Oh, what's the name of those stinky little paints?"

"Testors?" Ethel asked.

"That's right, Testors! And she painted Jackie + Danny— her husband's name—not the postman's—and drew a big heart around it right on the side of her mailbox. Her postman got the message and finally left her alone."

Ethel shook her head. Although Stan's visit was embarrassing, she was thankful that it had only been him and not Don Gardner.

Chapter Fifteen

They were delicious. Some of the best I've ever tasted. Ethel was encouraged by Stan's review. As soon as the Scrabble girls left, she set all the ingredients on the counter for the Caramel Pecan Frosting.

She remembered to add a quarter cup of butter instead of the tablespoon the recipe called for. His *not very sticky* comment didn't worry her. If the sauce was indeed a winner, she could always add corn syrup later to make up for that factor.

Following the instructions in the cookbook, she brought the frosting to a boil, but instead of topping a chocolate cake, she again poured the mixture into the bottom of the Pyrex pan. Then she carefully set the toasted pecans and cinnamon rolls on top. After the rolls had risen for an hour, she slid the pan inside the preheated oven.

While a cup of coffee warmed in the microwave, she dialed Quinn's cell phone. In the afternoon, he had a one-hour block when he just sat in his office.

"This is Quinn Benton."

"Quinn, it's Ethel." She pictured him with his feet propped up on the desk, staring at Katherine's picture.

"Hi, Ethel." She loved the way his voice brightened upon hearing hers.

"After the mailman comes today, I'll pop a sticky bun in the mailbox for you. On your way home from work, you can pick it up. You know, just like a fast food window. Make sure and put the flag down, so I know that you got it."

"Okay, Ethel." He chuckled. "Remember Harold, my elderly tenant?"

"Yes." How could she forget Harold? Only a few months ago, she'd accidentally delivered cinnamon rolls to his side of the duplex instead of Quinn's.

"I told him about your little contest, and he said with us in the neighborhood, there's no reason your grandson should have to eat a whole pan all by himself."

"Tell him if he wants to be a taste tester that he has to give an honest review."

"I explained that and, he said he'd be happy to oblige."

Just like that, her kitchen had three taste testers. "That's wonderful. I'll pop two sticky buns in the mailbox for you. Oh, and, Quinn, our mailman's name is Stan. Stan the mailman."

"That should be easy to remember."

"It has been! Life would be so much easier if everyone's name rhymed with their profession."

He chuckled.

"Make sure and tell Harold that his honest opinion is very important to me."

"I will. I'll call you tonight with the results."

The phone rang a few hours later.

On her way through the kitchen, Ethel paused to glance through the window above the sink. The little red flag on the mailbox was down. The caller might very well be Quinn.

"Hell-o," she said into the receiver.

"Ethel . . . I'm at Harold's, and we just enjoyed your uh . . . rolls with coffee." Quinn's voice was garbled a bit by someone grumbling in the background—probably Harold.

"Oh, what time did you drive by?"

Muffled exchanges were made.

"What was that, Ethel?"

"I asked, what time did you drive by?"

"I was there about 4:45, 4:50. Ethel, uh . . . Harold wants to speak to you. Uh . . . here he is."

The *uhs* . . . were not like Quinn. A knot tightened in her gut. While the remaining pan of sticky buns in the kitchen looked glorious, the tone in his voice reminded her that looks could be deceiving.

"Ethel . . ." Harold's gruff voice said. "I thought sticky buns had frosting and raisins?"

"No." She laughed, relieved that was all it was. "You're thinking of cinnamon rolls."

"I see . . . so these are what you call sticky buns? Hmm . . . I didn't know what I was signing myself up for."

"If you want, I can take your name off of the roster." His grumpiness surprised her.

"No. It's good to be challenged. Gives me something to do besides watch television."

"How can I improve, Harold?" She inhaled deeply, readying a pen.

"Well . . . Ethel, these weren't anything fabulous. I thought they were store-bought, you know, out of a wrapper."

"Uh-huh." She wrote *store bought* on the sticky note.

"They tasted like they were outdated. You know, when something's completely lost its flavor?"

"Harold, give me the phone," Quinn said in the background.

"No-oo. Harold, tell Quinn that I appreciate your . . . uh . . . honesty."

"Hey, she said it's all right." Harold only half-covered the receiver. "She says she can handle it. She's tough. She wants the truth."

Muffled voices followed.

If the sticky buns tasted like they were from an outdated wrapper, why had Stan raved about them? It was the same exact recipe.

"Ethel," Harold's voice returned on the line, "if these were sticky buns, they weren't sticky. And they weren't special. Mediocre at best."

Hand on hip, Ethel studied the air. Harold's review was a complete opposite to Stan's sentiments of *Delicious . . . Some of the best ever.* In all fairness, she hadn't stressed to Stan how important his opinion was. Although he'd been spot on about one thing—*they weren't sticky.*

"I appreciate your honesty, Harold. It's important."

"Wait a second. Quinn needs to hear this, too."

There was a pause before Quinn's deep voice returned. "Hi, Ethel."

"I just told Harold that I appreciate his honesty. It's important for the contest."

"I'm glad he didn't hurt your feelings."

The soft note of concern in Quinn's voice was worth all the harassment.

"Here, Harold wants to speak with you again." As he transferred the phone, Ethel heard him whisper, "Be kind."

Harold cleared his throat. "When's round two?"

Even though she felt like tossing in the towel, she summoned a giggle. "I'll have to find a new recipe, Harold, and I'll let you know."

She should call Joyce and bow out on the grounds of temporary insanity. Except, on account of the contest, everyone in the Scrabble group was craving sticky buns. Betty had even had a dream about one, most likely because of her low salt diet. If Ethel quit, the girls would never let her forget it. Not that it mattered.

Then, she recalled Joyce's *Ethel King, you can't even bake a boxed cake* comment from the fair. That alone inspired her to pick up the phone and dial her neighbor's number.

"Hello-o," Joyce answered.

"Joyce, it's Ethel." Already, she was losing her gumption.

"Hi, Ethel."

Ethel peered at Jimmy's chicken scrawl on a nearby sticky note. "You don't happen to know someone who could tutor in spelling?"

"Well, there's my niece. She's going to school to be a teacher. She's bright, very bright. She takes after my side of the family. Who's it for, Ethel?"

"Jimmy." She unloaded the truth.

"Jimmy? He doesn't know how to spell?"

"I found something he wrote." This was hard to admit to Joyce. "He spelled tried t-r-i-d-e and again a-g-e-n."

"Oh, my! I'll speak with my niece."

"Thank you." It would be nice if Jimmy could spell better by finals.

"Joyce, the other reason I'm calling," Ethel forced herself to proceed, "I'd like to bow out of the sticky buns contest. I don't know what I was thinking when I accepted the challenge." In the silence that followed, she recalled her earlier motivation. She'd been thinking about getting Joyce's dinner roll recipe. That had been the impetus behind her insanity.

"Ethel, you've never been a quitter."

"Maybe . . . before sticky buns."

For a moment, there was silence.

"I'm sticky bun challenged," Ethel admitted.

"Well, you used to be cinnamon roll challenged, and look at what happened there."

"You didn't tell me how hard it is to even find a sticky bun recipe."

"You're not quitting."

Joyce was getting close to hanging up on her. She could hear the receiver descending to the cradle. "Joyce, I quit!" It was Ethel's turn to almost get the receiver halfway to the cradle.

"You can't. All of your friends heard you," she said super fast.

"Watch me."

"Besides . . . once you master them, Ethel," Joyce's voice was sing-song now, "they really aren't hard. The toughest part of sticky buns for you will be finding the sauce recipe. You already have the cinnamon roll part figured out."

Ethel inhaled and felt a little Pettigrew pride trickle through her veins. "Well, I still should never have accepted the challenge."

"But you did." Ethel could just hear Joyce lowering the phone again. And before she could summon another thought, the line went dead.

Chapter Sixteen

Thursday morning after Jimmy left for work, Ethel set a frozen loaf of bread dough in the microwave to thaw. Then she sat down at her Formica table to read chapter three of Galatians. *Store bought. Completely outdated. Mediocre at best.* Before she'd be able to focus on her study, she had to get Harold's comments out of her head.

Maybe Gladys would pray for her.

She rose from the table, and at the curio cabinet, dialed her older sister's number.

"Hello."

"Gladys, it's Ethel. How are you?"

"Good. There are a few estate sales listed in the paper. I've been trying to figure out my route for tomorrow morning. How are you doing with your sticky buns?"

"Terrible, according to my taste testers."

"Taste testers?"

"Yes, I have four taste testers now. All men and bachelors." She included Stan, even though she wasn't sure of his marital status. "Last night, my sticky buns weren't even sticky."

"You should try Grandma Leona's caramel corn recipe. That sauce is sticky."

"I love that recipe. That's a great idea."

"Just don't boil it for the entire five minutes. Maybe only one or two. I think that's what makes it so thick."

"Thanks, Sis. Please, keep me and my sticky buns in prayer."

"I will."

Feeling renewed, Ethel returned to her Bible study. In Galatians chapter 3, she found her nugget for the day. *So, in Christ Jesus you are all children of God through faith, for all of you who were baptized into Christ have clothed yourselves with Christ.*

Wow! She could dwell on that all week.

She closed her Bible and got out her recipe box and studied Grandma Leona's caramel corn recipe. Butter, brown sugar, corn syrup, vanilla, and salt. Had she unearthed a great sticky bun sauce?

An hour later, Ethel slid a batch into the preheated oven. While they baked, today's sticky buns filled her home with the smell of victory.

Everyone showed up for Scrabble at eleven o'clock, including Joyce—with another plate of Parkerhouse Rolls. It was her third Thursday in a row, and she probably considered herself a regular member by now. On account of the buttery, melt-in-the-mouth rolls, she was probably right.

"How do we play partners with five?" Sharon asked.

"It'll have to be three against two. And, the only two that can handle it are," Mildred bobbed her pen back and forth between Joyce and Ethel.

An hour later, Joyce and Ethel led by fifty-six points.

"On Saturday, my granddaughter and I went to a Tom Hanks movie," Sharon said. "And, Tom Hanks was playing . . . some . . . body." Her voice trailed off.

"Ethel, have you been baking today?" Joyce asked. "I thought I smelled cinnamon."

"Cinnamon?" Ethel swallowed.

"Yes, cinnamon."

Everyone sniffed the air.

"If you can't smell cinnamon, dementia's on its way." Betty shook her head.

"Did you say *smell* cinnamon or *spell* cinnamon?" Sharon asked.

"I said if you can't *smell* cinnamon, dementia's on its way."

"Where'd you read that?" Joyce asked, turning the board toward Sharon.

"I can't remember. I probably heard it somewhere." Betty shrugged.

"I've heard it, too," Mildred said. Her daughter was a CNA, so she was probably right.

"Ethel, do you have any cinnamon?" Sharon asked. "We could all have a sniff and see how our snuffer's doing."

Of course, she had cinnamon; she was in the middle of a sticky bun contest for goodness sake. And, according to her taste testers, cinnamon was one of the top two most important ingredients.

"Yes, I have cinnamon."

The doorbell dinged.

Not again.

Ethel stared at her letter rack. *Don't be Don Gardner.*

On account of her company always parking in back, a person could easily think that she was home all alone, minding her own business, doing crossword puzzles . . . baking, not hosting a Scrabble party with four busybodies.

"Ethel, your doorbell dinged," Mildred droned.

What was it about Thursdays?

"Do you have your hearing aid in?" Betty crooked her neck like a squash, looking at her.

"She doesn't need one." Joyce moved letters around in her rack.

"She does today," Mildred said.

Sharon eyed her. "Ethel, didn't you say you have 20/20 hearing?"

Ethel had had enough. She swiveled in her chair, rose to her feet, and started for the door. She was a grown, mature woman with twelve grandchildren. She could handle this.

"It's 20/20 vision, not 20/20 hearing." The ebb and flow of Joyce's voice told Ethel her neighbor was right behind her, but instead of the door, Joyce veered to the window. She called, "Yep, it's the same Mercedes I was telling you girls about."

Mercedes . . . It must be a solicitor because she didn't know anyone with a Mercedes. Ethel was so relieved that she swung the door open wide.

Don Gardner stood on her porch wearing light-colored trousers, a green-and-blue checked shirt, and a grin. He had one hand relaxed-like in his front pocket while his other hand gripped a potted twig. Old Spice Cologne wafted through the screen.

With a swish of her arm, Ethel flung the door closed.

Her feet remained fixed while she stood staring at the white-painted door. Of all days to not check the peephole first.

"Ethel, who in the world was that? A solicitor?" asked Betty.

"No, it was some type of man, I saw him," Sharon said.

"That was a little abrupt, even for you, Ethel," Mildred's voice sounded like she'd managed to turn in her chair.

"It's that gardener guy I was telling you about. The one Ethel was puttering with in her garden."

Why in the world had she ever asked Joyce to sub at their Scrabble party?

Ethel inhaled deeply. She would handle Don's visit in a mature way because she was a mature woman. She was seventy-one years old, for goodness sake.

Ever so slowly, she opened the door, poking her head around the side.

Don was still standing there, holding the potted twig like it was a glass of lemonade.

"Ethel, I have to admit that was a new experience for me." He leaned toward the screen. "Shall we try again?" He managed a slight grin.

"Hi, Don," she said, glad he had a sense of humor. "I have my Scrabble group here." She hoped it explained her odd behavior. She joined him on the porch and pulled the door closed behind her. "We're all widows and, well, there're five of us today." Maybe he'd already guessed that she didn't trust a one.

She glanced toward the lace curtained window behind him.

"I'm sorry to interrupt your game. The reason I stopped by . . ." His gaze traveled to the crown of her hair before lowering to her eyes.

Was it the first time he'd seen her without her hat? She'd brushed her hair this morning before she'd vacuum cleaned. Hadn't she?

"Do you remember the blue-ribbon rose at the fair?" Don asked.

"Yes, the gal was a friend of yours." It had been one of the most beautiful red roses that she'd ever seen outside of a magazine.

"This is a cutting from her stock." He glanced to the potted stick of old rosewood in his grip. "You'll need to keep it watered until you're ready to plant it. And, with the average frost date for this area already behind us, you'll need to get it in the ground soon." He handed her the little pot which she gripped with both hands.

Up close, she could see that little green leaves had started to uncurl. It was her very own baby blue-ribbon rose.

"Thank you." As she peered up into his sparkling gaze, words evaded her. "This is so . . . so . . . thoughtful of you." To his right, a flash of white hair caught her eye before the lace curtains swished.

"Shirley gave me some starts."

She was glad he'd kept one for himself. Don's thoughtfulness, teamed with her swishing the door in his face, made her feel terrible. "I . . . I wish I had something to give you." She scanned her front yard. But if he had access to blue-ribbon roses, there probably wasn't much there that he'd be interested in.

"Do you like sticky buns?"

"What kind of question is that?" He rocked back on his heels, grinning.

"I've been experimenting." Their time was limited, so she'd tell him the story condensed. "Do you remember Joyce, my neighbor?" He nodded, while she continued. "Well, shortly after the fair, she challenged me to a Sticky Bun Baking Contest. I've never made them before and finding the right recipe has been far more difficult than I anticipated. I'll give you one to take home, but there's something I need you to do for me . . ."

He entwined his hands in front of his lean waist and rocked back on his heels again. "Yes, of course, Ethel. Anything. Anything at all."

His sentiments were vaguely familiar, reminding her that Edwin had spoken such lyrics to her once . . . fifty years ago, before they were married.

Don must like her.

The poor man thought she was a Best-of-the-Fair baker. Little did he know that she was a fly-by-the-seat-of-the-pants baker. Maybe, after today's sticky bun, he could attest to that himself.

"Um . . . if you could call and tell me what you did and didn't like about the sticky bun, I'd appreciate it."

"I can do that, Ethel." A soft smile lit his lean face.

But how could she get the sticky bun to him? She didn't want him to meet all of her friends. They'd gab on forever about flowers. Ask him to smell the tin of cinnamon that they'd nabbed from her cupboard. And, they'd think Don was cute and tease her until her dying day.

"Walk through the side yard," she pointed south, "and meet me at the back door. We'll make the handoff there."

"Okay, Ethel." The apples of his cheeks bunched and he blinked several times in succession.

When she closed the front door behind her, Betty scampered to her chair.

"Would you look at that, I drew a . . . K," Joyce said as if it was a wonder letter.

"What haven't you been telling us, Ethel?" Mildred made a quarter turn in her chair.

Even though Ethel tried not to draw attention to the picture window behind Joyce, out of the corner of her eye, she couldn't help but notice the shiny gleam of Don's head as he followed the widely-spaced stone steps through the side yard.

"What'd he give you?" Betty asked.

"A baby rose." Ethel carried it toward the kitchen.

"Who is he, Ethel?" Sharon asked. "Joyce said that he's your flame from the fair."

Joyce! She forced herself to keep moving. "He's not my flame. Don's . . . simply a gardener friend of mine." Ethel set her baby rose on the counter. Then using a spatula, she transferred one of today's sticky buns onto a paper plate and wrapped it in foil.

"Oh, I knew he looked familiar. Don Gardner, he . . . uh, goes to my church," Betty's voice trailed off.

"Oh . . ." Ethel grabbed a pen and wrote on a nearby sticky note: *Call me and tell me what you think is wrong with it.*

As planned, Don was waiting for her at the back door.

"Thank you again. I've never had a blue-ribbon rose before." She smiled, making the transfer.

He could have easily said, "I know." Instead, he simply met her gaze. "I'll call you tonight."

He wasn't being presumptuous. That's what she'd asked him to do.

"If you don't have any intentions of marrying him, Ethel," Joyce eyed her, "You need to be careful with this one."

What did she mean? *This one.*

"He's a widower. His wife passed away a little over a year ago," Betty said.

"He told me," Ethel said.

"Don and I go to the same church—God's Garage. We meet at Moscow Auto Body," Betty informed Joyce.

"I've heard of your church," Joyce said. "Folding metal chairs in the bay area, grease on the floor, and . . ." She rolled her eyes.

"Girl calendars on the wall," Mildred added.

"Yes, not all of the mechanics are saved, but the owner is. They're not nasty calendars, just . . ." Betty fluttered a hand toward her chest, "showing a little too much, you know . . . We try to focus on the preacher."

Ethel clamped down on the insides of her cheeks, stifling a giggle.

"What's Ethel's new flame like?" Joyce reached into the letter bag.

"He's not my flame."

"But . . ." Sharon turned to stare at her. "Joyce said you were arm in arm at the fair."

The only reason Don had taken her arm was to get her away from Joyce. Or had it been the cookbook lady— Marlene Flanagan?

Joyce appeared to have a selective memory, as well.

Betty waved a hand. "I don't know Don personally. Only that he and his wife used to sit two rows in front of me at church. She had short, white, curly hair, and she often wore a light blue cardigan. Then she got ill, and they didn't come to church for a couple of months. And then he was back all by himself. I know too much, girls." Betty played a *D* after "place" and turned the board for Joyce's turn.

"What do you mean?" Ethel asked, as curious as the rest of them.

"He carries two Bibles now and sets one in the chair beside him. We're all pretty certain that it's her Bible."

A hint of cinnamon in the air and the tiny clicks of Betty setting tiles in her rack followed.

Ethel knew just how Don felt.

"That says a lot about the man." Sharon glanced at Ethel.

"It sure does." Even Mildred agreed.

"Men have a harder time after they lose their spouse than women do," Betty said, thoughtfully. "They don't have the camaraderie and friendships like we do."

"Nope, they only have the TV." Sharon sighed.

Maybe they were right. Don was lonely.

The first time he'd seen Ethel, she'd been wiping at her eyes, if not crying. Don had been in tune with her pain because he was also hurting. She now felt bad about slamming the door in his face, being so awkward, and having him meet her at the back door.

Don was in need of a friend. Hopefully, that's all he was looking for.

Chapter Seventeen

Jimmy washed up at the sink while Ethel poured glasses of milk. "I'm sorry it's only grilled cheese sandwiches and tomato soup. We'll have the sticky buns tonight as dessert instead of appetizers." She giggled. Earlier, she'd grabbed a warm, sticky pecan and it had tasted delicious. "The Scrabble girls didn't leave until three o'clock today. Then I took a little nap, and the afternoon got away from me."

"Grilled cheese sandwiches are the best." Jimmy sat down in his usual seat, and they gripped their hands and said the Lord's Prayer together.

Afterward, Ethel asked, "How was your day, honey?"

"Okay. How come there're only three today?" He eyed the nearby pan of sticky buns.

"I gave rolls to Quinn, Harold, and the gardener guy." She gave her glasses a nudge. "How was work today?" Was he avoiding the question?

"You never did tell me how it went with the aphid control man." He took a large bite of sandwich.

"He said I have a real problem." Ethel shrugged and took a sip of milk. "He emptied an entire bottle of spray in just the front beds. I wouldn't be surprised if he called in the near future to . . ." her ankle bobbed nervously beneath the table, "schedule the side yard."

"What's his name again?"

"Don."

"Don . . . What's his last name?"

"Don . . . Delta Don." Ethel shrugged. "Does it matter?"

"No." Mouth bunched, Jimmy shook his head. "Except Quinn said you were acting oddly the other night."

Lowering her chin, she regarded him. "What went wrong today at work, honey?"

A dullness entered his gaze, and the corner of his mouth twitched. "Remember when you and Mrs. Purtell were at the shop?"

"Ye-es, of course."

"Vance still has me doing the Tile Check every evening." His shoulders rounded slightly. "My friend, Matt, he's a lawyer student."

Lawyer student? Surely, that wasn't the way Matt described himself.

"Matt said that Vance usually only hazes the new guys a couple of days."

What? Jimmy had started work there three weeks ago, today. She thought about the Polaroid picture and the little note she'd written and mailed to Bill Hicks. Would it make a difference? Would the busy man even care?

"Have you ever done or said anything? Argued with Vance in any way?"

"No. I've always been very respectful."

"Then he's a bully."

The somberness in Jimmy's eyes suctioned all of the grandma stuffing right out of her.

"Vance, my boss, has been humming this old tune." Jimmy took a bite of the sandwich and solemnly chewed. "He must have talked to Mike, the Lewiston manager. How else would he know?"

"Know what?" Had she missed something?

"It's nothing to brag about, Grandma, but . . ." He folded his arms on top of the table and sighed. "Three years ago when I first started at Bill's, I was just this scrawny kid. You know, I never played football. Bill's Tires was the first time I ever really had to use my muscles or had ever been a part of a team."

Though it took restraint, she resisted the urge to smile.

"From the start, the Lewiston guys knew." The corner of his mouth twitched. "Somehow, they could see right through me. Whenever I'd walk through the showroom, they'd sing "I'll Make a Man out of You." You know, from the movie *Mulan*."

Ethel tilted her head. "I don't think I've seen it."

"You're kidding?" He stared at her.

"Is Clint Eastwood in it?" It sounded like something he'd say.

"No." He chuckled. "I have it here. We'll have to watch it sometime—after I'm caught up on my studies, that is. Anyways, Vance hums it now whenever I'm around. It doesn't matter that I'm one of the fastest tire changers he's got." Jimmy's broad chest expanded as he shook his head.

So, the song had followed him all the way from Lewiston.

"Grandpa would be proud of me, though, for the way I'm handling my boss. Do you know what I'm talking about?"

"No."

"I just tell myself to let it all roll off my back like a duck."

Grandparents do live on.

"That's what your granddad always told you kids."

He nodded. "I remember him saying it a lot."

"You'll show 'em, Jimmy. You might not have had muscles in the beginning or grit." She wiped tears onto the shoulder of her T-shirt. "But, Bill's Tires is *making a man out of you.*"

He nodded like he was truly listening.

The phone rang in the other room.

She was almost tempted to say *don't answer it.*

"I'll get it." Jimmy rose from his chair.

"No, let me get it."

"It's no problem, Grandma."

Ethel set a hand on the green-swirled Formica table and swiveled her legs around. Her grandson was nimbler than she was.

"Hello, King's residence. This is Ethel's grandson speaking."

Ethel swiveled back around to face the table. It could very well be Quinn or Harold, but her gut told her it was Don. She lifted her gaze. In the windowsill sat the pot of old rosewood that would someday bear blue-ribbon red roses. Maybe she should plant it in the side yard where she'd have a nice view of it from the kitchen window. She'd only have to move a clump of daisies. She'd do that tomorrow before the weather changed.

"It's for you, Grandma." Jimmy returned to his seat. "It's Don... Don *Gardner.*" The light in his eyes told her that he thought he had something significant to share with Quinn.

Maybe he did, and maybe he didn't.

"Hello, Don. What did you think of the sticky bun?" Because Jimmy could hear every word said, she'd try and keep this as business-like as possible.

"Hello, Ethel. It had good flavor."

"Uh-huh." She nodded.

"I hadn't had a sticky bun for quite some time."

It had been quite some time since she'd had one, too. "Good flavor. And . . . ?" Maybe she was finally onto something. The sticky pecan she'd tried had been delicious.

"They were sticky," Don said.

"They were?" Had she, Ethel King, finally mastered the *sticky* in sticky buns? She raised a fist into the air in a silent hallelujah.

"Yes, stickier than I remembered."

"Uh-huh." She waited for his praise to continue.

"Have you tried one, Ethel?"

"No, my grandson and I are saving ours for after supper."

"Oh, it sounds like I've called during your dinner hour. I'm sorry."

He was so sweet about it, but . . . now was her chance.

"That's all right, Don. I'm glad you enjoyed it. Have a good evening."

"Uh, you, you, too, Ethel."

Click.

She felt sixteen again, trying to politely end a call with an admirer.

Or had she been polite? Maybe she'd been a little too abrupt like Katherine.

She set the kettle on the stove for decaf coffee. "That was Don. He liked the sticky bun. Said it was sticky."

"Good."

"Yes. Sticky is a very good sign. Maybe we're almost there." Ethel set dessert plates on the table.

The phone rang again in the other room.

"That's probably Quinn, calling with today's sticky buns report." Ethel returned to the living room. "Hello." She held the receiver against her ear, smiling.

"Hello, Ethel."

It sure sounded like Don. But, he seemed too polite to call twice in the same dinner hour. "Quinn . . . is that you?"

"Yes. I'm at Harold's. Do you have a pen?"

"Yes." She grabbed a pen and a nearby pad of sticky notes.

"Ethel, have you tried them yet?"

"No, but, I did try one of the pecans."

"They're sticky this time. Harold thinks you may have put in too much corn syrup. Here, wait a second, he wants to speak with you."

Too much? It had only been a quarter cup.

Harold's gruff voice came on the line. "Since Quinn's not man enough to tell you, it's gonna have to be me."

"Okay, Harold, I'm ready." She blinked, readying her pen.

"You just lost the prize, Ethel. Something went way wa-aaay wrong. When they're heated, the sauce is like a gooey cement, if it's at all cool, it is cement. Almost broke my tooth."

"I'm sorry, Harold." Could she believe him?

"My teeth stuck together so tight, it was like I had lock jaw. I wrote a note for Quinn to call 911 but he got a putty knife instead. Don't worry, Ethel. I can move my mouth now."

Ethel forced herself to swallow.

"He's only teasing, Ethel," Quinn bellowed in the background.

"Thank heaven," she murmured.

"It was sticky enough it loosened my upper plate. I'll send you the bill."

Was he exaggerating again? It was hard to tell.

Don had tried to warn her. *They were sticky. Have you tried one yet?* But, she'd been in such a rush to get off the phone that she hadn't asked him to elaborate.

Why in the world had she accepted the challenge?

"I'm sorry, Harold."

"To be honest, Ethel, you could save us all a lot of grief—"

"Harold!" Quinn said loudly in the background.

"She appreciates my honesty."

"Yes, but not your discouragement."

"Now, listen here, Quinn. This is my—" An arm-yanking, muffled sound followed.

Clunk!

The receiver sounded like it had dropped three feet in the air and landed on Formica. Was Quinn grappling with his eighty-some-year-old neighbor?

A thump of cabinetry followed.

"Quinn! Now, you two boys stop that! Stop your horsing around this instant," she said even louder.

No one answered. There was only heavy breathing and the shuffle of chairs on old hardwood.

"I mean it. You boys stop, or you're both fired." That probably wasn't enough incentive. "Stop or . . . or . . . I'll call the police."

"What's going on?" Jimmy was now in the doorway.

"They're fighting. Quinn and his eighty-year-old neighbor. Over my sticky buns!" Ethel said without covering the receiver.

Jimmy chuckled and then retreated.

"We're fine, Ethel," Quinn's voice volleyed like he didn't have a grip on the phone. "And, except for the sauce, we enjoyed them."

"Quinn . . ." She tried to be loud enough for them both to hear. "I appreciate Harold's honesty. How can I improve if nobody tells me the truth?"

"Did you hear that?" Harold mumbled in the background. "She's tough."

There was a clunky sound, and then the line went dead.

Slowly, Ethel returned the receiver to the cradle.

She chewed on a knuckle and staring at the phone, waited for one of them to call her back. Then, she moved to the kitchen doorway.

At the table, Jimmy held half of a sticky bun in one hand and a glass of milk in the other.

"Don't eat the sticky buns!"

"I kind of like them." He swallowed.

"Don't!" Ethel covered her eyes with both hands, trying to get her wits about her. "Should I call 911? They're fighting."

"No-oo." He chuckled.

"I'm calling them back." She returned to the phone. She couldn't remember Harold's last name. Otherwise, she'd look him up in the directory; but she knew Quinn's cell number by heart.

His phone rang twice. "This is Quinn."

"Are you boys all right over there or should I call 911?"

"We're fine. I'm just leaving." There was the click of a door closing. "I just learned what a half nelson is." Quinn cleared his throat. "When Harold was in the Navy, he used to wrestle."

He was serious.

"What is it?"

"Well . . . he grabbed my arm, and then he crooked his arm behind my neck in such a way that I couldn't move."

It wasn't a pretty picture.

"I hope my sticky buns haven't hurt your friendship."

"No. Harold seemed pretty pumped about the evening."

She sighed. "In the future, Quinn, you don't need to defend my baking like that. I mean, they're just sticky buns. He didn't insult anything I can't change."

"Ethel . . . Wow! There's wisdom in what you just said."

"Don't sound so surprised." She managed a giggle. "Have a good evening."

"You, too," he said softly.

She hung up and with a sigh, wished she'd never agreed to the challenge. Tonight's 911 Sticky Buns had almost sent Harold to the hospital. And they'd also almost prompted a call to the police. She, Ethel King, was sticky-bun-challenged, and the time had come to do something about it.

Chapter Eighteen

Ethel's hair looked terrible, so she put on her gardening hat—the one with the plastic strawberries on the side—and tied the bow beneath.

"Where are you going, Grandma?" Jimmy turned in his seat at the table.

"To Joyce's. I told you not to eat the sticky buns." A second one was in his grip.

"The flavor's great." He chewed with one eye half-closed. "But your teeth stick together when you—" His mouth locked mid-word.

She couldn't watch. She hoped he had dental insurance.

She started down her back steps, went out the side gate and then east. Across Logan Street, Joyce's boxy, white, single-level home sparkled in the evening sunlight. Joyce was as meticulous about the exterior of her home as she was the interior. Only yesterday, she'd been outside Windexing her mailbox and the latch on her gate.

Ethel started up the front walk to her neighbor's red front door, glossy as fingernail polish. Not one little smudge, chip or bubble blemished its surface. She rang the doorbell so she wouldn't leave a mark.

Help me, Lord. Help my words. Help my heart—

The door swung inward, and a glorious smell drifted out and dawdled right under Ethel's nose. Right in front of Joyce, she was tempted to close her eyes and take a big old whiff.

"Hell-o, Ethel . . ." Joyce's dark penciled brows furrowed.

Ethel inhaled deeply, trying to pinpoint every last ingredient. Cinnamon, butter, toasted pecans . . . and something she couldn't quite decipher.

Sticky buns were undoubtedly in the oven.

Pulling the door closed behind her, Joyce joined her on the covered front step. She wore a royal blue apron—the same color as the ribbon she'd been after much of her adult life.

"Ethel, I was just thinking of you. I spoke with Bridget, my niece, and she said that she'd help tutor Jimmy. It's something she can put on her resume, and she'll only charge minimum wage."

"So, she's a good speller?"

"Ye-es." Joyce waved a hand. "She's going to be a teacher. But, she can't start until January." Joyce deadheaded a nearby potted geranium. "She has too full of schedule this semester. And she said that evenings would be best."

"Not till January? I suppose that'll have to work." Now, she only had to break the news to Jimmy.

"The reason I'm here—" Ethel gave her glasses a nudge and swallowed.

"No, Ethel."

The woman knew her too well.

"I'm tired. Burned out."

Joyce rose to face her. Mouth pursed tight; her chin scrunched up like a little ball of dough. "It's too late to bow out now."

Since the minute when Joyce had first challenged her, it had been too late to bow out. Ethel had heard the serious note in her voice, even then.

"I'll tell you the recipe. That's what you want, isn't it?"

"I haven't been perfecting my sticky buns for the last *week* to have you bow out now." Joyce's voice shook with preheated emotion.

Try the last month . . . Ethel bit her tongue. There was more to it than just winning the recipe. On account of the ribbon, Joyce wanted to beat her and in front of her friends.

"You can't quit. I've perfected something wonderful in there." She motioned a hand in the direction of her kitchen. "Stan told me they're amazing! The best ever."

Stan the mailman? Ethel wasn't so sold on his taste buds.

"You're not quitting!" There wasn't a drop of love in her neighbor's steel-green eyes. Only revenge.

And, it hurt.

Lord, did you see that? Ethel swallowed hard, trying to stomach the blow. *Please, tell me that You saw that. I'm trying, Lord.*" She drew in a breath. *I'm really, really trying. But... do I have to love this neighbor?*

Ethel didn't know what kind of face she'd been making during her long-winded prayer. But, Joyce frowned, went inside, and flung closed the door.

Ethel stared at the perfectly manicured door and mouth dry, forced herself to swallow. This must be how Don felt that day. He'd just been standing on her front porch, holding that baby blue-ribbon rose, and dreaming of the delight that would be in her eyes.

It had taken a man with a large heart to respond the way he had when she'd reopened the door.

Joyce reopened the door.

"Hi, Joy-ce." Ethel sniffled. "Shall we try again?"

"You're so weird sometimes." Joyce heaved a sigh. "It's my turn to say I'm sorry first, for once, Ethel. You've always been my favorite neighbor. And you must know, I want to beat you more than anything in the world because of that *huge* ribbon you won. You, of all people." Joyce swallowed tears. "So, do your best. Go ahead and pray about it if you want, and I'll pray, too. And may the best sticky buns win." Joyce didn't smile, but she held her head a little higher as she gazed at her through her gold-framed glasses.

"Whatever happens, Joyce, let's not lose sight of twenty years of friendship."

Joyce batted her eyes and nodded.

Ethel started down the walkway and setting a hand on top of the picket gate, paused. Across the street, evening sunlight filtered through her weeping cherry tree in the southeast corner of the yard, casting little slits of rainbow sunshine everywhere. It looked magical. From here, you'd never know that her flowers were infested with aphids. In the evening light, her home with its white picket fence and colorful autumn garden appeared nostalgic and quaint.

"Ethel . . . Ethel!" Joyce called out.

Ethel turned to look over her shoulder.

"You're a dear, dear friend." Hands gripped beneath her chin, Joyce truly meant it.

Ethel blew her a kiss. Then, after looking both ways, she ambled across the street. Ethel didn't need to practice making sticky buns anymore. In her heart, she knew she shouldn't win. Joyce had all of herself rolled up in those buns. For some reason or another, her friend needed the validation of winning more than Ethel ever had.

No, the only thing Ethel needed to work on was her apology to Don Gardner. She'd been on the other side of the door now and understood a little better how it had felt that day to be in his shoes.

Jimmy piped whipped cream over the surface of his morning coffee. While he'd been upstairs studying last night, Grandma had thrown the last sticky bun in the garbage. They weren't that bad. A bit gooey-gluey, but he'd liked the flavor. The taffy-like sauce reminded him of a Sugar Daddy, one of his favorite candies.

"I spoke with Joyce last night." Grandma patted the corner of the table.

"Uh-huh."

"We've found you a tutor." She dangled her spoon above her bowl of Fiber One cereal, smiling at him.

"Oh." He didn't know she'd been looking for a tutor for him. "For what?"

"Your spelling, honey."

"I don't need a tutor, Grandma." He chuckled. Ever since Mrs. Harmon got a hold of him in fourth grade, he'd been a pretty good speller.

"I found your little song that you wrote upstairs." Grandma nudged her glasses higher up the bridge of her nose and smiled softly at him.

What song upstairs? His gaze roved the boxes of cereal, stored on the counter to the right of the sink. Had he brought any of his songwriting with him?

"You know, 'Baby, Don't Brake Me,'" she said.

He laughed out loud. Somehow, the ballad that Kenny, Allison's nine-year-old brother, had written must've ended up in his stuff.

"Where'd you find it?" He blinked, curbing a smile.

"I wasn't going through your things." She clasped her hands above the table. "You see, the first week you moved in, your mother called. You'd accidentally grabbed their Visa bill in your pile of paperwork. And, that's when I found the song. Don't worry; I only spoke to your mother and Joyce about it. Your spelling, not the Visa bill."

"Mrs. Wooten?" His spelling might have already gone very public. "Grandma, you thought I—"

"Jimmy! It's nothing to feel ashamed of." Her voice softened. "But, you need help. Four-year schools are known for being harder than two-year universities."

She meant well.

"Grandma . . . I—"

Shaking her head, she patted the table between them. "Joyce's great-niece is going to be your tutor. She's going to college to be a teacher. She'll be able to put this on her resume."

Put what on her resume? Teaching a college student who already knew how to spell . . . how to spell? *Hold on a second . . . Mrs. Wooten's great niece?* His memory rolled in reverse to the neighbor's white Ford Taurus and the guys in the bay yelling *Goodyear.* And how time itself had slowed as the morning sunlight trailed behind her pageantry on her walk to the door.

"Wha . . . what's her niece's name?"

"B . . . Buh . . ." Eyes narrowed, Grandma chewed on her lower lip. "Bridget! She'll be your tutor. Don't worry, honey. I told Joyce that I'd be the one to pay for your sessions."

He lowered his glass of milk to the table and swallowed.

"I can pay, Grandma. I mean, it is my . . . uh . . . problem."

She shook her head. "Bridget has too busy of a semester right now, but she can start in January. I told Joyce, I'd discuss it with you before we planned any further."

"Uh . . . evenings are best. They're all the same to me."

"I'll tell her you're flexible."

Had he written anything down that day in front of Bridget? He didn't think so.

"One thing I can say about you, Jimmy," Grandma smiled softly, "you've always been so agreeable. More than Katherine, that's for sure."

"Thanks." He curbed a grin. It was easy to be agreeable when things were completely and utterly going your way. Someday, he'd tell Grandma and reimburse her. In the meantime, he needed to find the song and study Kenny's third-grade spelling.

When the phone rang that evening, Jimmy was still at work, so Ethel set aside her crossword puzzle and hurried to answer it.

"Hello."

"Ethel, I'm calling about tonight's sticky buns." The deep voice on the other end of the line sounded like Quinn's.

That's right. She'd left two rolls in the mailbox, raised the flag, and left a message on his cell phone. The day had been a blur. That morning, she'd thrown several ingredients in a pan—butter, brown sugar, a couple of tablespoons of cinnamon—melted it and called it a sauce. Sticky bun baking had become a habit for her now.

"Yes . . . Quinn."

"Here, give me the phone," Harold grumbled in the background.

She inhaled, trying to prepare herself.

"Ethel, it's Harold. I don't know what you did or what you're thinking, but you're not going to win any prizes with today's batch."

Harold obviously hadn't heard about the booby prize. Who was she trying to kid? She was a terrible baker. Joyce had always been better. Joyce needed to win. The mailman was proof that Joyce would win.

"They're gritty. What'd you put in the sauce? Sandpaper?"

"Cinnamon."

"Cinnamon?"

"Yes, cinnamon. You guys have been bugging me about cinnamon."

"Have you tasted them?"

"No."

"Wha-at? Why do we have to taste them if you don't?"

"Okay. Hold on a second." She set the phone down and ambled into the kitchen. She folded back the foil and using her bare hand, tore a chunk off of the nearest roll and popped it into her mouth.

The addition of cinnamon to the sauce was like grit on the tongue and was surprisingly strong. One bite was all she needed. Jimmy could have the rest. She washed her hands before returning to the phone.

"You're right, Harold. They're terrible." Nothing fazed her anymore.

"What's going on over there? Defend yourself."

"Give me the phone." Quinn was already grappling with him. If they weren't careful, cabinet thudding sounds would soon follow.

Ethel cleared her voice. "Have you heard . . . Harold, how this all started?"

"What do you mean *this all*? Do you mean the contest?"

"Yes, the contest. My cinnamon rolls miraculously won the second best of show at the fair this year, and because of that, my neighbor Joyce challenged me to a Sticky Bun Contest. Harold, the silver-ribbon truly was a miracle."

In the silence that followed, she pictured him nodding.

"Uh-huh," he finally said.

"God was in the kitchen with me that day." She didn't know if Harold was a believer. They hadn't talked about God the one time they'd met when she'd accidentally delivered cinnamon rolls to his side of the duplex.

"Do you think God was with you today?"

"Oh, He's always with me. It's just that I think Joyce, my neighbor, really deserves to win this time."

He chuckled for a moment right into the phone. "Sounds like you're caving into the pressure, giving up." Then his voice sounded a bit muffled like he hadn't completely covered the receiver, "She's throwing in the towel."

Was she? For some reason, maybe habit, she'd gone ahead and baked sticky buns today. But her heart hadn't been in the task, and Harold could tell.

"Joyce has been my neighbor for twenty years. She's always been the baker. And, while everything turns out glorious in her kitchen, I've always been the seat-of-the-pants baker." Ethel sighed. "Besides, I don't need to win. Not like her. She needs to. It's that important to her."

"Oh, I see. She's proud. Is that what you're telling me?"

Ethel peered into the mirror. *Joyce was proud.*

"She needs to win. Something at the very core of her needs the validation of winning."

"It's called pride. And, if I've ever heard nonsense, I've heard it today." Harold's voice climbed Moscow Mountain at the end. "I'm going to give you a word of advice." He paused for a long moment like the word had temporarily escaped him. "Fortitude . . . You've lost your fortitude. The battle's only begun. You can't quit now. If it means that we have to eat sticky buns every day between now and . . . when's that contest of yours?"

"October 17th. Next Thursday. My Scrabble group always meets on Thursdays."

Harold sighed. "In less than a week, Ethel, this will all be behind us. Now, here's some advice for the days ahead: Caving into inferiority on account of another man's pride is not acceptable on land or sea."

She thought about saluting, but he wouldn't be able to see her anyway. "Thanks, Harold. I needed a pep talk. Except, I don't like the idea of baking sticky buns every day or even once a week for that matter. I'm burnt out."

"Our role isn't easy either, Ethel. But, we're all in this together."

That was easy for him to say, but still, Ethel felt inspired.

In the kitchen, she grabbed a pad of sticky notes and penned her grocery list: butter, brown sugar, flour, cinnamon, pecans. Then she took a moment, giving her nose a chance to remember what the faintly familiar ingredient had been that had wafted from Joyce's oven to the front porch. She couldn't quite place it.

On a separate sticky note, she wrote *Fortitude* and stuck it to the front of the fridge.

"Fortitude." While she thought she knew what it meant, she wanted to be certain, so she grabbed the Scrabble dictionary out of the napkin holder on the table and thumbed through the Fs. *Fortitude, n.* Oh, it was a noun. Hmmm . . . *The strength of mind that enables one to endure adversity with courage.*

He was right. Somewhere along the way, she'd lost her strength of mind. But, thanks to Harold, she was back in the kitchen.

Chapter Nineteen

Tuesday at noon, two days before the contest, Ethel answered the phone.

"Hello."

"Grandma . . ." It was Katherine.

"Yes, honey . . .?"

"This is Katherine." Her granddaughter sounded unusually concerned.

"I know." Did she think she'd said *Yes, honey* to everyone who called? "How are you? Are you enjoying your job?"

"Yes. I'm on break," Katherine lowered her voice to a whisper. "I'm glad I'm here for only one semester. How are you, Grandma?" Again, the sweet note of concern.

"Oh, same old, same old around here." Though Ethel tried to sound like her same old self, a little airy note crept into her crackly voice. "Except, I've been baking up a storm. More like a Hurricane Ethel than a Julia Child type of storm. And sadly, sticky buns aren't as easy as the Scrabble girls led me to believe." An anxious knot formed in her gut. "Our contest is in two days, and I still haven't mastered sticky buns."

"Aren't they just a caramel sauce with pecans and cinnamon rolls on top?"

"Yes, but finding the right sauce is a whole 'nother matter. Besides, I'm tired of baking. I'm more of a gardener. I always have been." Ethel gazed toward the front windows and through the lace eyed her pink-eyed Susans.

"Well, I'm sure the judges at the fair would disagree with you this year." Katherine laughed softly. "The reason I'm calling is Quinn's coming over for dinner Friday night, and I wanted to get your meatloaf recipe. He loves your meatloaf."

"Oh, I didn't know that your little place had a stove."

"It does. It's the old, skinny, white enamel-type with an oven that's about a foot wide."

"Lucky for you, it's wide enough for a loaf pan."

"Barely."

"While I have you on the phone . . ." Ethel noted movement across Logan Street and moved to the picture window near the table. Stan the mailman placed a small parcel inside Joyce's box.

Just then, her neighbor's front door flew open, and Joyce bustled down the walkway toward Stan, a plate of something in her grip.

Oh, if she only had a pair of binoculars! Ethel smooshed her cheek against the glass.

Some kind of transfer was being made.

Words were exchanged.

Joyce even pointed toward Ethel's house, maybe her mailbox.

Stan tipped his hat and, with the paper plate in hand, walked across the street.

"Grandma? I'm still here." Again, there was an unusual note of concern in Katherine's voice.

"Have you ever been to Ireland's?" Ethel asked. "I keep hearing about their sticky buns."

Stan strode by, feasting on a sticky looking roll.

"That's because Ireland's Café is a landmark. Their sticky buns are regarded as the best on the Palouse, which may be the perfect misnomer as very few restaurants on the Palouse offer sticky buns."

Misnomer. After Stan delivered her mail and headed west, Ethel returned to the curio cabinet to write the word on a sticky note, so she'd remember to look it up later.

"I'm confused, Katherine, are you saying Ireland's are the best or . . . ?"

"If you don't have anything planned, Grandma, I could meet you at Ireland's in about an hour for a little research. We have an early-release today at school."

"Oh! That would be wonderful."

"It'll be good to see you. Remember to bring your meatloaf recipe."

"I will, honey."

During the next half hour, Ethel wrote out her recipe, changed into a clean button-up shirt, and brushed her hair. Then she took a loaf of Rhodes dough out of the freezer to thaw for this afternoon's batch of sticky buns. And, right before she left the house, she decided she better leave a note for Jimmy, in case he came home early for some reason or other.

While she penned the message, she was tempted to write *Gone to Ireland with Katherine*, but she didn't need to worry the poor boy. Heaven only knew that between going to school and plunging tiles at Bill's Tires, he had enough worries. So, she was a good grandma and wrote the correct title for the local landmark. *Gone to Ireland's Cafe with Katherine.*

Sixteen miles north of Moscow, Ireland's Café was located on the left side of Highway 95, right before the turnoff for downtown Potlatch. Mid-afternoon, the little yellow café was surprisingly busy. Ethel sat across from her granddaughter in a booth. Fresh off of work, Katherine wore a white shirt with a pointed collar, black tailored slacks, and high heels. With her blond hair pulled up into a sassy bun, she looked sharp and professional. The twenty-eight-year-old U.S. history teacher probably had half the boys at Potlatch High School in love with her. Maybe all of them.

With a coffee decanter in one hand, their middle-aged waitress set a warm sticky bun, and an extra plate on the bright yellow table. Matching Ethel's vivid recollection, Ireland's sticky buns filled a dinner plate. An abundance of buttery sauce puddled on top and dribbled down the sides.

"Whenever I mention *sticky buns*, everyone asks if I've been to Ireland's," Ethel told the waitress.

"Best buns on the Palouse," she said, setting more napkins on the table.

Katherine caught Ethel's eye and smirked while the gal poured coffee into the white mugs with a three-leaf clover on the side.

Over the bun's vast topography, Ethel only counted six and a half pecans. Maybe Ireland's carried the only sticky buns on the Palouse.

Katherine divided the sticky bun in half, and Ethel's half was still large enough to be dinner. She dabbed her finger in the sauce and was surprised to taste only butter and brown sugar. "I thought there'd be cinnamon in the sauce. The guys keep telling me to up the cinnamon."

"They probably mean inside the rolls. Too much cinnamon in a sauce can taste gritty."

"Yes, like sandpaper." Ethel thought it healthy that she could already giggle about Harold's response.

Using a fork, she savored her first bite. "They are good." Swishing her mouth around, she detected a faint sourdough aftertaste. She peered around at the busy café and the other patrons. Surely, Ireland's didn't employ the same method she did. She giggled to herself and took a sip of coffee before asking, "How are you and Quinn?"

"Good. But, he's worried about you." Katherine leaned toward her and spoke slowly. "He said when he calls, it's like you don't know it's him."

"Oh . . ." Holding the mug against her mouth, Ethel tried to hide her amusement. Katherine was fishing for information. Quinn must have told her about Don's phone call and how awkward she'd acted that night. That's probably why she'd wanted to meet today. That, and the recipe.

"Grandma, that's not like you." Leaning forward, Katherine took her hand. "Do you think you might need a hearing aid?"

Were they sincerely concerned or just trying to get her to talk? She studied Katherine's large, blue eyes.

"Is there any chance you've had a stroke? He said you've appeared flustered lately."

They were fishing deep. *Flustered* was entirely different than hearing loss. They were trying to wriggle the truth from her. Although, there wasn't much to tell.

"No, honey, tell Quinn that my ears and mind are just fine."

The bell on the front door jangled and Ethel was only too happy to divert her attention to the two men who'd entered.

One was middle-aged, behind him stood a younger man she'd seen somewhere before. Maybe in her living room . . . or on TV. Was he a movie star? No. She lowered her fork to her plate. Oh, pooh! He was Katherine's foot doctor.

"What is it, Grandma?"

"Doctor Brad's here." Ethel felt her stomach sink. Was it purely coincidental or were the two meeting on the sly? What an awful thought.

Katherine sat back in the booth. Her mouth hung slack, and she didn't turn to look over her shoulder.

Instead of the bright Hawaiian shirts that Brad had worn last summer, the sandy blond, European-looking man wore a sage-green sweater and dark slacks. Minus the bold prints, he appeared far easier on the eye.

"Ethel . . ." Brad recognized her first, probably because Katherine's back was to him.

"Doctor Brad."

He stopped beside their table. "Kathe . . . rine . . ." His voice hadn't been breathy like that when he'd said Ethel's name. His Adam's apple bobbed in his neck while he gazed at her granddaughter.

He still had feelings for her.

"Hi, Brad. Small world." Katherine's fake diamond earrings made her eyes appear extra sparkly.

"We're on our way home. They have us practicing in Coeur d'Alene once a week." He nodded toward the older dark-haired gentleman who'd gone ahead to snag a seat.

"So, what brings you ladies to Potlatch?"

Sticky buns came to mind, but Katherine beat her to the punch. "I'm subbing here at the high school for a teacher who's on maternity leave."

Too bad she'd told him so much information. Now, Brad might look her up and discover she was living here alone, seventeen miles away from Quinn.

"I see. Good for you. And, how's your foot?" The young doctor's gaze drifted to her bare left hand.

"Great. No problems."

"Good to hear." His gaze shifted to Ethel. "It's nice to see you both."

Ethel nodded before he finally stepped away and slid into a seat, two booths behind them. Sadly, he'd have a view.

"That was awkward," Katherine whispered behind her coffee cup and then lowered it to take a sip.

They enjoyed the sticky bun for a while in silence. The caramel sauce was rich and buttery.

"Did you remember the recipe?"

"Yes, I wrote it out for you." Ethel snapped open her purse, then slid the card across the table.

"Thanks. Quinn loves your meatloaf."

She'd actually voiced his name out loud, maybe even loud enough for Brad to hear if he had extremely good hearing.

Ethel's memory returned to Paradise Ridge and watching the sunset with Quinn—one of the most wonderful men in the world. She hoped her granddaughter still thought so. Did she? Ethel didn't like the way she was fanning her face with the three-by-five card. Twenty-eight was too young to be menopausal.

Even though she wasn't finished, Ethel set down her fork and placed her hands in her lap.

"What is it, Grandma?"

Heightening the tension, Ethel cleared her throat. "If you were shipwrecked on a desert island, who would you rather be there with . . . Quinn or Doctor Brad?"

Katherine's eyeballs bulged. "Grandma . . . you said that a little too loud!"

"Did I?" Ethel pressed her fingers to her lips. What an awful thought! She lifted her chin, and for a moment, just listened to all the babble in the busy cafe. There were so many people talking, surely, Brad couldn't have overheard her crackly old voice?

"You're just avoiding the question." It was just like Katherine to be creative.

"No." Katherine shook her head. "I think you need a hearing aid."

"And you haven't answered me." Getting on a personal level with Katherine was often like playing tug of war with a snake. "Should I repeat the question?" Ethel nudged her glasses higher up the bridge of her nose.

"No!" Katherine's mouth pursed tight. "Think about it, Grandma. It's an easy answer."

Ethel tapped her fingers of her right hand on the yellow laminate and thought about her question. *If you were shipwrecked on a desert island, who would you rather be there with . . . Quinn or Doctor Brad?* What was there to think about?

"Who?" she asked.

"On a desert island"—leaning forward, Katherine whispered, "a doctor would be far more valuable than a U.S. history professor."

It felt like a fork to the heart.

"If you were going to be shipwrecked for years," Ethel clarified, "possibly even decades, and had to live off coconuts, and maybe even have a few babies—"

"Grandma!" Katherine's cheeks flushed the same shade of red as the nearby bottle of Tabasco. "Do you know how many women still die during childbirth in third-world countries?"

"Kath . . . rine . . ." Ethel had almost forgotten how awful she could be. "You're lucky to even be alive. You're lucky you survived the shipwreck." Gripping her hands in her lap, Ethel leaned forward. "What I meant is . . . if you could be—"

"Grandma! *Lower* your voice." Katherine whispered with exaggerated pronunciation.

Maybe her hearing was going.

"If you could be shipwrecked with *anyone* in the world," Ethel whispered, "not because of their skills, but because of the way you *feel* about them." She tried to stress that point. "Who would you want it to be?"

Only a few months back, Katherine had sobbed buckets for Quinn Benton. Didn't she remember?

Her granddaughter's gaze finally softened, and she was good about keeping it locked on Ethel's and not letting it veer at all to her right.

"I've missed you, Grandma." She smiled. "If I could be shipwrecked with any *two* people in the whole world," Katherine held up a finger to keep her from interrupting. "I'd want it to be Quinn and you. So, brush up on your survival skills." She fluttered the recipe card in front of her face like a fan. "And, bring this recipe."

The café was very busy for having only one waitress on staff. Doctor Brad got up and grabbed the coffee decanter from behind the counter. After he'd filled up his cup, he topped off other customers' cups at nearby tables before moving to theirs.

"You girls want a refill?" He peered at Ethel, first.

She set a hand over her cup. "Not after two o'clock for me."

Katherine pushed her mug toward him.

Ethel was glad it was only a three-leaf clover on the side of the mug, and not a four. Under the influence of infatuation, men often read into everything.

"How was the sticky bun?" he asked while pouring.

"Really good. Grandma's in a sticky bun baking contest, and we're actually here for research."

That's what she should have told him the first time he'd asked.

"They really should be called Tricky Buns. They're trickier than you think. I like their sauce," Ethel said. Except just a hint of something was missing. Had she been onto something with her caramel corn sauce? The pecan she'd tried had been delicious. What if she hadn't added the corn syrup?

"They might give you the recipe if you ask." Brad gripped the near-empty decanter in one hand.

"I doubt very much." Ethel shook her head.

"I'll ask for you." Without waiting for her response, he returned the coffee pot to the burner behind the counter. From there, he gripped the lip of the serving window and leaned his head inside. "I have a question." He must have got the go-ahead, for he soon proceeded through the swinging doorway into the kitchen.

Ethel sighed and looked at Katherine. Brad was trying to be her knight in shining armor for her granddaughter's sake.

"Grandma . . ." Katherine jabbed a thumb toward the kitchen.

From the other side of the serving window, Brad waved her over.

"What in the world." Ethel swiveled her legs out of the booth. She smoothed the back of her cardigan and followed Brad's lead behind the counter and through the double shutters. A long metal-looking grill took up the majority of the kitchen area.

A young woman wearing a shower cap stood holding a spatula.

"The sauce is easy," she told Ethel. "It's a 2:1 ratio. Two parts brown sugar to one part butter. That's it."

"Oh." Just like her caramel corn recipe. "How much butter?" Ethel couldn't believe her luck.

The young cook pointed to a pan shelved above the grill. It was at least three, maybe four times the size of a nine-by-thirteen. "A pan that size takes two pounds of butter."

"Two pounds!" Ethel breathed.

Brad chuckled. "Only six thousand calories in butter, alone."

"And with sticky buns, the more sauce, the better," the young woman whispered.

"The more sauce, the better," Ethel said.

"That's all I can share. The dough is a secret family recipe."

Secret family recipe? Had Ireland's also stumbled upon the aged whipping cream for their sourdough? Surely not. The little cafe had been in business far too long. People would have put two and two together by now. Did they sell Beano at the register?

Ethel thanked the cook and then glanced at her benefactor. "Thank you, Doctor Brad." She made sure to keep his title intact. Just because he'd unearthed Ireland's sticky bun sauce, she didn't want him thinking he could move other mountains.

Inspired by her visit to Ireland's, Ethel went home and started her sauce. She melted one stick of butter in a saucepan and stirred in one cup of brown sugar. Then wanting a little more zip, she borrowed a few ingredients from her caramel corn recipe and added a half teaspoon vanilla and a quarter teaspoon salt. After a good stir, she poured the mixture into the bottom of her square glass pan.

Her stomach knotted. Here, it was two days before the contest, and she was still experimenting.

Two hours later, Ethel retrieved today's mail, and set two foil-wrapped packages of sticky buns in the box, and raised the flag. Not wanting to take any chances, she stuck a note that read: *Stan, these are for Quinn* to the front of the mailbox.

She sorted through her mail on the way to the door. Fingerprints on the back of the Latah Credit Union envelope were proof that a postal carrier should not eat sticky buns during his route. Someday, she'd address the matter with Stan. In the meantime, she held the envelope beneath her nose, took a deep whiff and detected cinnamon and something else.

What was it?

She set her mail atop the pile on the curio cabinet and then dialed Quinn's cell phone. After three rings, it went to the recorder. "Hi, Quinn. It's Ethel. Sticky Buns are in my mailbox for you and Harold. Call me tonight with the results and NO fighting!" And, then suppressing a giggle, she hung up.

Chapter Twenty

Jimmy took a break from plunging floor tiles to stretch his aching back. Vance stood behind the counter reading something, and under his breath, he hummed the all-too-familiar tune from *Mulan*.

"Vance, why don't we have popcorn?" Jimmy asked over his shoulder.

"'Cause Les Schwab has popcorn."

"Yeah. Well, Les Schwab also has tires."

"I just work here." Vance scowled.

He seemed even more uptight than usual, not a good combination with how wired Jimmy felt. He placed the plunger in the center of the tile and hummed "I'll Make a Man out of You," along with his boss. Then he lowered his knees until the rubber head was deflated and the suction tight before lifting up.

While he stepped to the next tile, Jimmy glanced over at the lone customer in the reception area. Half of a white bushy brow and eyeball peeked around the side of the newspaper at him. You know that you looked like a doofus when customers didn't want to be caught looking at you.

By the time Jimmy neared the front counter again, he had another question for Vance. "Why don't we give our customers anything at Christmas? Everybody loves getting gifts at Christmas."

"'Cause we're not Santa."

"Do you know . . ." Jimmy lowered his voice, "that Les Schwab gives away steaks and says *Merry Christmas*? They even have a toy drive for needy kids."

"You have to buy tires to get a free steak, Dimmy."

Jimmy blinked. Had he meant to call him that?

"Yeah, well, what do we do?"

"We have a basket of candy canes." Vance pointed to the counter like they were still there. "And when they leave, we say *Merry Christmas*." He flicked a hand for Jimmy to get back to plunging.

"Where's the Christmas spirit in that?"

Vance tipped back his head and, palms up, petitioned the ceiling.

"We got the best location in town, Dimmy." He had meant the name. "We don't need to advertise. Now, would you . . ." Vance mouthed "shut up?" and pointed to their customer.

"Sorry," Jimmy whispered.

"What'd your grandmother do, put too much fabric softener in your shorts today?"

"No." He started in on the next row of tiles. "She doesn't use fabric softener."

Vance had a good point. Bill's was located in the heart of Moscow, while Les Schwab was practically hidden on the east side of town behind the Safeway. But, Les Schwab's advertising more than made up for their location. Only last night when he'd been watching the news with Grandma, there'd been Les Schwab ads on the TV, not to mention their full-color newspaper insert that he'd used as a placemat for today's morning cereal.

Over his shoulder, he waved for Vance's attention. "We might have a better location in Moscow, but Les . . ." he pointed east— "Schwab" he whispered, glancing at their customer, "is getting right in our homes selling tires."

"I've had enough of your funny business." Vance tossed the comics he'd been reading onto the counter. "I'm gonna call Bill and let you tell him your ideas yourself. Better yet, you can talk to his wife. She handles the advertising."

"No, that's all right. I've heard that's a quick way to get canned." Jimmy's stomach knotted. No one was to ever call Bill or his wife directly with ideas. You were supposed to go through the chain of command, even if your boss was missing a link or two.

"You've wasted enough of my time. It's time you wasted some of theirs." Vance held the phone out toward him, dialing the number.

If he refused would it mean a yellow slip?

The fellow in the reception area rustled the paper as Jimmy made his way to the counter. He was sure getting an earful today.

"Hi, this is Vance at the Moscow location. Is Peggy Hicks in?"

He hadn't imagined things. Vance did not like him.

Holding the phone out, Vance mouthed *take it.*

Jimmy gripped the receiver to his ear and heard a clicking sound as someone picked up on the other end.

"This is Peggy."

"Hi, Mrs. Hicks. This is Jimmy King from the Moscow location." Crud, he was still holding the toilet plunger. He passed it to Vance. "Um . . . I was discussing with Vance, our manager here, a few ideas that I had for advertising."

Vance ground the heel of his steel-toed boot into the toe area of Jimmy's steel-toed boot.

Maybe he shouldn't have mentioned Vance's name, but if he were going down, he'd do his best to take his boss with him.

"I don't know if it's a good time for you to talk," Jimmy said.

"I have a few minutes." She sounded tired.

"Well . . ." He gulped. "I wish we sold popcorn. I mean *had* popcorn in a little red trolley, you know, like Les Schwab. A few people—customers—have told me that having a snack like that would help pass the time. Take their mind off the wait. And the salty, buttery popcorn smell might mask some of the rubber in here." He was probably talking too fast; he tried to slow down and take a breath.

Vance tipped back his head and was holding his gut like he found Jimmy's sentiments hilarious.

"They were very disappointed when they were here that we didn't have popcorn. I know this probably sounds corny, but for some reason or other, they thought all tire places had popcorn. And by the time they got here, they were craving it."

"I see." She sounded a little more awake now.

He didn't know if he should proceed, so for a five-second stretch, he just listened.

"Do you have any other ideas . . . Jimmy?"

"Do I have ideas?" He grinned, then glanced at Vance's sobering expression.

An ugly look that went deep had replaced his boss's earlier mirth.

The man did not like him.

"Well, ma'am, I live with my grandma here in town while I attend the U of I, and she has this Polaroid camera." He couldn't look at Vance anymore, because he was half laying on the counter now, smothering his mouth so hard that he looked like he was going to pop.

Jimmy turned his back to him. "She likes to take pictures of me with my car. I was just thinking the other day that every guy I know values a picture of himself with *his* car. I thought if we had a Polaroid camera in the showroom, we could take pictures. One for the customer with their car and their new tires, and one for our files.

"We could staple the photo in our customer file, and when say, a Mrs. Purtell was coming in for an appointment, we could look in the file and know what she looked like. The minute she steps through the door, we could greet Mrs. Purtell by name."

"Jimmy . . . I'm going to tell my husband about your ideas." Her voice sounded brighter now, almost friendly.

"Thank you, Mrs. Hicks. You. . . you have a nice evening. Goodbye." Jimmy smiled and reaching past Vance, who was now standing, hung up the phone.

"You're *tiring* me out, Dimmy King. Put that in your little file." The ugly look returned. "Now, get back to work."

"Yes, sir." Jimmy returned to tile plunging. Vance was tired of him. Really tired of him. So tired of him, he might try and can him without a yellow slip. But, according to Matt, the lawyer student, Bill's Tires couldn't fire him without a reason. For the corporation's protection, it was best to have a trail of yellow slips.

After he'd finished the row, he turned and plunged his way back toward the counter. His stomach babbled with hunger. He sure hoped Grandma had made another batch of sticky buns today.

"Jimmy . . . Jimmy King."

He glanced up. But it wasn't Vance who'd called him. Nope, for some reason, his boss stood eyes wide, face pale, the comics clutched in one hand.

"Jimmy . . ."

The deep voice had been off to his left, from the customer area.

He slowly turned his head ninety degrees. White-haired, at least fifty, and wearing snakeskin cowboy boots, Bill Hicks tossed his newspaper on the coffee table. The founder, president, and owner of six Bill's Tires locations rose to his feet. Even though he was a foot shorter than Jimmy had imagined, he'd still recognize the man anywhere. He looked exactly like the picture that was hanging in the hallway on the way to the restroom. If the man grew a goatee, he'd look like Colonel Sanders's twin, just skinnier.

"Jimmy, man the front counter for us. Vance, I'd like to have two words with you in the back room."

"Yes, sir," Jimmy said. Then, pausing, he counted on his right hand. "You're fired," was two words.

With his heart pounding in his ears, Jimmy stood behind the counter and watched the two men make their way to the backroom. After Bill had two words with Vance, Jimmy sure hoped he didn't want to have two words with him.

Maybe Grandma had contacted Bill. Maybe she'd sent him a picture of Jimmy tile plunging, and Bill just had to see it to believe it. Then again, Vance might just be getting a talking to, and Jimmy was the one getting fired for all of his goofy ideas.

It was all Grandma's fault.

The popcorn. The picture. In spite of all of Grandma's goofy ideas, he was tempted to dial her number and ask her to pray.

He couldn't do that. The guys might come back any minute and catch him talking to her.

I am with you always.

Grandma's little note from God served as a reminder to pray.

Lord, he breathed, *I really like working here. I like Matt and Ted. And, You know me. I'm a simple kind of guy. I could work here for the rest of my life and be happy if that's what You want for me.* He inhaled deeply and hoped that's what God wanted for him. *And, Lord, it's really hard to get on at Les Schwab or probably any other tire place, for that matter, when you've been fired from your other tire job.*

He swept the reception area and behind the front counter, Windexed the glass doors, and tidied the magazines on the coffee table.

A few minutes later, Vance carried his lunch pail and his coat over one arm and, without even glancing Jimmy's direction, exited through the front doors. Instead of using the wide steel handle, he put his hand right on the sparkling clean glass.

"Matt," Bill's voice carried through the showroom.

Pale-faced, Matt jogged out of the employees' lounge onto the floor. Everyone was on Bill alert.

"Yes, sir."

"Man the counter for us while I have two words with Jimmy."

Two words.

While Jimmy followed Bill to the backroom, he felt the color drain from his face.

"I think you know why I'm here today, Jimmy." Bill crossed his arms and leaned back against a box of paper towels.

Bill had already said a whole lot more than two words in a country-hick kind of way.

"Is it because of a Polaroid picture?"

"Yes, it is." Nodding, Bill reached into the chest pocket of his Western shirt. "Have you seen this?" He handed him a photo.

In the left corner of the picture, in a blue muumuu, Grandma's friend Sharon hammed it up for the camera. "No, not this one." Behind the counter, Vance looked right at the camera while, plain as day, Jimmy plunged floor tiles.

"Your grandmother mentioned in her letter that Vance has been hazing you. It took a while to get to the bottom of it, but we finally did. Come to find out, Vance has a nephew with a different last name, who we were looking at hiring here right before you requested your transfer."

"But . . . Bill's doesn't ever hire family at the same branch." Jimmy repeated the company bylaw.

"That's always been our policy." Bill nodded.

That's why Vance never liked him.

"I like how you handled a tough situation, Jimmy."

Tough situation?

"You were being bullied, and you showed him who the better man was."

He let Bill's compliment sink in like butter on mashed potatoes.

"What are you studying at the U of I?"

"Business, I think."

"I think you have a knack for advertising."

Jimmy shook his head. "I wouldn't want to be behind a desk all day. I love what I'm doing right now."

The corner of Bill's mouth twitched. Then lowering his chin, he studied him with sparkly eyes. "I've been looking for an employee like you. Someone who can serve as a liaison between our ad department and the sales floor. An idea man. Take some marketing classes and think about a future here with us."

Bill wasn't firing him.

Bill Hicks liked him.

"Yes, sir. I will, sir. Thank you, sir." Jimmy sunk his teeth into his lower lip.

"In the meantime, I want you on the floor, selling."

"That's fine with me—"

"You're personable, friendly, and, I like how clean-cut you are. Our customers appreciate that."

"Clean-cut? Does that mean no beard?"

Bill nodded. "When you work in sales, no facial hair's allowed."

"My grandma will like hearing that." He tried to look at the bright side.

"I can't tell you how many little old ladies have called to complain about facial hair." Bill chuckled.

Knowing Grandma, she'd probably been one of them.

Chapter Twenty-one

Ethel poured two glasses of milk and then set the jug off to her left at the table while Jimmy washed his hands.

"Grandma, I have some good news to tell you," he said over his shoulder.

"Oh, wait until you're sitting down." She clasped her hands together, giggling and tried not to let her mind wander.

Jimmy sat down and eyes unusually bright, smiled over at her. And, then prolonging the agony, his gaze drifted to the pan of sticky buns in the center of the table.

"What's your good news?"

The phone rang.

"Oh-h!" Her hands dropped to the table. "What terrible timing!"

"I'll get it." He scooted back his chair.

"Thanks, honey." Oh, what did he have to share with her? To kill time, Ethel transferred a beautiful sticky bun to her plate and reminded herself that looks could be deceiving.

"It's Quinn." Jimmy returned to his chair.

Ethel locked eyes with him. "You're only allowed to eat one." She held up an index finger. "I need to take notes. And this one's mine." She pointed to her plate.

"I promise not to touch it." He grinned.

In the living room, she picked up the phone. "Hello, Quinn."

"Hi, Ethel. With the contest being only two days away, we knew you'd be antsy about the results."

"Ye-es, I'm *antsy* to get this all over with. I'm tired of making sticky buns." After Thursday, she wouldn't care if she saw another sticky bun in her life.

"Well . . . Harold thought it would be helpful to give you a blow-by-blow account."

"Okay."

"Harold's taking his first bite."

"Tell her I'm using a fork," Harold said in the background.

"He wants you to know that he's using a fork. Now, he's chewing, and looking up at the ceiling. He's taking a sip of coffee."

"Tell her it's tasty."

"Ethel, Harold said it's tasty."

"Uh-huh. How sticky are they?" If this batch wasn't sticky, she was up a creek.

"Wait a second. He's taking another bite."

"Tell her . . ." In the background, Harold sounded like he was talking with his mouth full this time and, she didn't even try to decipher it.

"Harold said he likes that it doesn't make his mouth stick together."

She suppressed a hallelujah. "But are they sticky?"

"She wants to know if they're sticky. Wait a second, Ethel. Harold wants to speak with you. Uh… here he is."

The conversation felt all too familiar. Maybe it wasn't a hallelujah batch. She inhaled deeply.

"Ethel . . ." Harold's gruff voice came on the line.

"Yes, hello, Harold."

"This is the one."

"Huh?"

"This is the one."

"Really?" That was all he was going to say? After all they'd been through—the cabinet thumping, the near-expletives, the lectures on fortitude, the almost 911 sticky buns . . .

"Uh-huh. This is the one."

"Well, then hallelujah!" She heaved a weary sigh. In the silence that followed on the other end of the line, she waited for him to make a disclaimer or an exception, or maybe a praise other than *tasty*.

"Quinn's taking a bite now. I hope your hands are clean."

"They are. Tell Ethel they are tasty." It was Quinn's turn to be in the background.

"Quinn said they're tasty."

"Tell her they're the perfect stickiness."

"Quinn said they're the perfect stickiness."

The side of her cheek bunched against the receiver while she beamed.

"Our work is done," Harold said.

"Thank you. Tell Quinn—"

Click. The line went dead.

She stared at the receiver in her grip. Harold had hung up on her. Probably not on purpose. He was probably so relieved that tonight was the last batch. Not that she could blame him, she was tired of sticky buns, too.

She returned to the kitchen and sat down while Jimmy finished pouring himself another tall glass of milk.

The sticky bun on her plate appeared untouched, but he'd already emptied the pan and his plate.

"Jimmy, I told you not to eat them all."

"I took notes for you." He pointed to a small slip of paper stuck to the table beside her plate.

She stared at the little yellow sticky note and his legible-enough penmanship.

There purrfect.

The message didn't click in her brain. It required deciphering. Then she remembered that Jimmy's spelling needed to be read out loud.

"They're perfect." She smiled at Jimmy. "That's what Quinn and Harold said, too, in not so many words."

"They were really good, Grandma. Perfect. Just like your letter to Bill Hicks."

Her lower lip curved inward and then she chewed on a corner of it. He knew about the letter. A hand flew to her mouth. Which meant he also knew about the Polaroid picture.

"Bill was in our store tonight. He fired Vance. And, I was afraid he was going to fire me, too. But instead, he showed me the picture that you'd taken of Mrs. Purtell and Vance *and* me plunging tiles.

"I was mad at you, Grandma, about being there, and not listening to me. But now I see God's hand in all of it."

She wiped a tear from the corner of her eye.

"I was telling Vance some of my ideas for advertising. I didn't know it was Bill Hicks behind the newspaper in the reception area." Jimmy's tone was low like it was his first time reliving it. "Vance didn't like my ideas, but Bill did. Bill wants me to take some marketing classes. He wants me to think of a future with Bill's Tires."

"I'm so happy for you, honey." Ethel crossed her hands over her heart and just held them there in silent praise.

Then she lowered her gaze to his little note and was thankful that God in His infinite wisdom had her grandson live with her first before Bill Hicks put him in charge of the company's advertising. They needed a few years to work on his spelling.

That evening, Ethel knew the time had come for her apology. She had a little wind beneath her wings, and she wouldn't put off calling Don any longer.

While Jimmy was upstairs studying, she flipped through the half-inch thick Latah County phone book and found Don Gardner on the first page of the Gs.

Donald wasn't a younger person's name. Anyone looking through the phonebook pretty much knew that a solo listing for a Donald Gardner who lived on Polk Street implied that he was elderly and lived alone.

While the phone rang, Ethel wrapped the curlicue cord around the fingers of her left hand and glanced at herself in the mirror above the curio cabinet. Her hair looked better than most days.

"Hello."

"Hello, Don . . ."

"Ethel, is that you?" There was no hesitation. He didn't have to guess which elderly woman's voice was on the other end of the line.

"Yes, Don, it's Ethel King."

"You're the only Ethel I know. No surname required."

She smiled. "I wanted to let you know that I got the little rose in the ground a day or two after you gave it to me."

"Good. Where'd you decide to plant it?"

"In the side yard, where I'll be able to see it from the kitchen window."

"Good. It should get a lot of sun there."

"It does. The other reason I'm calling," she pulled a chair away from the dinette set and sat down, "is I wanted to apologize for closing the door on you the other day."

A brief silence followed while her memory returned to the front porch and the wee smile on his face as he held the little potted rose.

"I understand. I embarrassed you. You had all your girlfriends over, and this old man showed up on your doorstep, unannounced."

She smiled at his ramblings.

"To be honest, Ethel, I've had many a chuckle at the memory."

She giggled with him for a moment and was glad that he was able to see the humorous side.

"Friends?" she said into the receiver.

Silence followed on the other end of the line, and she questioned if he'd heard her.

"Friends?" she asked a little louder.

"For starters."

She inhaled and peered down at the green shag carpeting. "Don. . . I can't commit to anything but friendship." She thought of Edwin's picture on her nightstand. She could never give up that picture or its placement. "You see, I'm still in love with my husband. I know he's not with us anymore, but I have too many memories of my Eddy." Tears pooled in her eyes. "But I can be a friend, Don, when you need one."

"Okay, Ethel." In the silence that followed, she imagined him nodding on the other end of the line. "That's all right. That works for me . . ." And in a very quiet voice that perhaps he didn't think she could hear, he whispered, "for starters."

Chapter Twenty-two

Thursday, October 17th

Just like the morning of the fair, Ethel had Jimmy knead the yeast dough before he left for school. While it rose, she made the sauce and poured it into the bottom of a nine-by-thirteen pan. Following the recipe that she'd used for the fair, she poured the aged-to-perfection soured whipping cream into the pan, and stirred. It was no longer the exact recipe she'd made last night. The addition of the aged cream made it unchartered territory.

"Oh, Lord, please make my sticky buns providentially delicious."

Ethel made the rolls with extra cinnamon and nestled them into the pecan-covered sauce. Lastly, she covered the pan with a damp tea towel for the rolls second rise.

And, then, so the girls wouldn't know what hit them, Ethel grabbed her purse and drove to Safeway for a layered bean dip and a bag of tortilla chips.

While she waited in the checkout line, she knew there was something else that she'd wanted to pick up when she was here. Something for the get-together today. What was it? Even though she racked her brain, she couldn't remember.

She drove home and parked in back. It wasn't until she was lifting the latch on the back gate that she remembered what it was she'd wanted to buy.

Beano!

Mildred swore the little pills worked like magic.

It was too late now to go back to the store. She'd just have to ask Mildred to share her Beano with everyone.

Ethel slid the pan of beautifully risen buns into the preheated oven. In less than twenty-five minutes, her little home smelled heavenly. Like a woman who'd been practicing sticky buns for a month, she flipped the pan onto a large platter. The dough was baked all the way through. The rich caramel-looking sauce wasn't too thin or too thick. But, the truth would be in the tasting.

As planned, Joyce arrived a few minutes early with a platter of equally beautiful sticky buns. They tented the platters loosely with foil so the girls wouldn't see them beforehand.

Mildred and Sharon arrived first. And, while they two ambled up the back walkway, Betty's Chrysler rolled in.

The back door creaked open.

"Oh, girls, the house smells so good," Sharon said, on her way through the kitchen. "Like sticky bun heaven."

"I smelled sticky buns as soon as I stepped out of the car." Mildred set a bag of Fritos on the counter.

"You're kidding!" Ethel dried her hands on a tea towel.

"Cinnamon and a hint of nutmeg." Mildred continued into the living room.

Nutmeg? In all of her experiments, Ethel hadn't thought of trying nutmeg.

"Ethel, did you use nutmeg? Never mind." Joyce waved her hands. "Don't tell us. We don't want anyone to know whose is whose."

Nutmeg had been the ingredient Ethel couldn't quite decipher that evening on Joyce's doorstep. She'd have to remember Mildred's keen sense of smell for future bakeoffs.

Not that she ever wanted to compete in another one. The sticky bun challenge had almost done her in.

Ethel wrote her name on the bottom of five paper plates and placed a sticky bun on top while Joyce did the same. To keep the contest as fair as possible, the judges waited in the sewing room while they set the plates around the Scrabble board.

"Mix it up, so *we* don't even know," Ethel said.

Without arguing, Joyce switched the sticky buns at each place setting, left and right, then left and right again, until it was difficult to tell whose was whose.

"You can come in now," Joyce yelled.

Sharon led the pack. "I've been craving sticky buns all week. But, I didn't want to drive all the way to Ireland for one."

"Ireland's," Joyce said.

"I know. I just thought it would be fun to say," Sharon giggled, taking her usual seat at the table.

"They look good, girls," Betty said.

Mildred held onto the back of her chair and sat down. "They look rich."

"May the best sticky buns win," Joyce said.

Ethel sat down in the chair beside Mildred. Her stomach felt too knotted to take a bite, so she drew a letter out of the bag to see who'd go first.

Using a fork, Betty took a bite from the plate on her left. "That's a bit salty." She usually had to watch her salt, but she was cheating today.

Mildred picked up her pen and wrote down the names of the Scrabble teams.

"I drew an *A*," Ethel said, which meant she'd play first. Then on account of the rules, she had to toss the *A* back into the bag and redraw seven letters from scratch. Luckily, she drew another *A*. She was able to spell "jake," getting rid of her *J* and *K* right off the bat.

"That's a proper noun," Sharon said. "Remember, Ethel, we can't play proper nouns."

"It's also an adjective," Ethel said.

"What's it mean?" Mildred peered over the top of her glasses at her.

"It means . . ." Over the years, Ethel had looked *jake* up enough times that she should remember. "It means . . . *satisfactory*."

"You finally know what a word means." Mildred's turn was next. "She pointed her fork to the sticky bun on her left. "That sticky bun is just *jake*."

"Yum-yum." Sharon tapped her fork at the plate on her right. "There's something about this dough."

"We didn't stage it left or right, girls," Ethel said. Too bad she hadn't chopped her pecans a bit; then she would have known whose was whose.

The girls were more into the Scrabble game than she'd expected and, for several turns, it was like they weren't paying any attention to the sticky buns at all.

"Whose turn is it?" Mildred asked.

"Mine." Sharon finally played an *O* on an open *X* for a double word score. "Eighteen points." Her shoulders did a little wiggle. She was getting smarter about the game. Or maybe her play was simply a fluke like Ethel's prizewinning cinnamon rolls had been.

"I agree with Sharon. This dough's lighter." Mildred motioned her fork to the bun on her right.

Joyce's chest rose, and her demeanor lightened.

"But this sauce . . ." The sticky bun that Betty had earlier thought was too salty, she now closed her eyes, savoring.

Ethel couldn't stand it any longer and took a bite from the sticky bun on her right. It was buttery and cinnamony. The combination of pecans and caramel just made you want to take another bite. She swished her mouth around, hoping for, and at last detecting, the slightest hint of sourdough. It wasn't as noticeable this time, maybe because of all the caramel sauce.

For her next bite, she tasted the roll on her left. The dough was noticeably lighter, but then again so was the sauce. She took her time, savoring the flavor, and detected the ever so subtle hint of nutmeg. Ethel curled her toes inside her pink fluffy slippers. She might be a little biased, but there was just something about her sauce that made her want to keep eating. Probably the half pound of butter.

"Whose turn is it?" Mildred asked.

"Oh, it's mine." Ethel studied the board. Their taste testers weren't into the contest as much as she'd expected. They wanted to keep playing, take their own sweet time, and enjoy the buns with their coffee, while she and Joyce sat on pins and needles.

After a long time spent studying the board, Ethel spelled "soda" for five points. She turned the board for Mildred's turn.

"I can't stand it any longer," Joyce said. "Someone, please vote."

For once, Ethel agreed with her.

"I like how light this one is." Mildred tapped her fork to the plate on her right. "The other one's too rich for me."

"I like how light this dough is." Betty tapped her fork to the right. "But I love this sauce." She pointed her fork to the plate on her left and kept it there. "They're both delicious, girls, but this one's more of a sticky bun in my opinion."

All eyes shifted to Sharon.

Sharon sat up straighter in her chair. "They're both delicious. But this one," she tapped her pointer finger to the plate on her right, "spells sticky."

Ethel didn't want to second-guess herself, but the roll on Sharon's plate reminded her a lot of how her rolls had looked dishing them out of the pan—sticky, with lots of coated pecans.

Joyce peered around the table. "For some reason, I thought there were going to be more judges here."

Betty shook her head. "This is all we've ever had in our Scrabble group."

"So that's it. All our work, Ethel, comes down to three taste testers. I'd sure like to have it be a little larger pool than this. Wouldn't you?"

Did Joyce think that she'd won? Or was she simply stalling?

When it really came down to it, Ethel was only guessing. She had no idea if hers was the wonderful dough or the wonderful sauce. It could go either way.

Joyce swiveled in her chair and began rapping on the window. "Stan . . . Stan!" Like a love-crazed woman, she bellowed behind the glass.

Mid-whistle, Stan, the postman, paused on the side of Ethel's white picket fence and looking their way, tipped his hat. Then he continued toward her mailbox and lifted the lid.

Joyce was on her feet, squeezing between the wall and the back of Sharon's chair before racing through the doorway. Had anyone been in the kitchen, she would have bowled them over. The back door didn't quite close behind her.

"Stan . . . Stan! We need another taste tester."

"Go out there, Ethel," Mildred said. "Make sure she's not telling him which roll to pick."

What an awful thought.

Ethel rose from her seat and hurried through the kitchen. Joyce could be bribing him at this very moment. *Pick mine, and I'll bake maple bars for you for the rest of my life.* Ethel swung the door wide.

"We're having our . . . sticky bun challenge today . . . and only three judges are here." Joyce sounded out of breath.

"That's a good number. Can't be a tie when there's only three."

"Three's not enough! We need four. Four's better," Joyce said over her shoulder.

"Hi, Stan." Ethel held open the door as he brushed past. "There's soap at the sink."

"Morning, Ethel." He touched the bill of his dark hat.

Joyce shuffled in behind him and held the towel like a maître d' while he dried his hands.

Stan joined the Scrabble group in the living room. Ethel and Joyce wrote their names on the bottom of two more plates and dished out their sticky buns. And then Joyce carried both plates to the table.

Betty, who'd given up her chair for Stan, now stood beside Sharon.

Joyce set down the plates and fork at the east end of the table, and her eyes did not dart or give away clues.

Stan didn't take off his hat, probably because he had postman hair. He ignored the fork, picked the sticky bun off the plate on his right and, like Jimmy, ate half of it in one bite. Then he set down the remaining half, chewed and peered up at the ceiling. Afterward, he rubbed the fingers of his right hand together thoughtfully. Next, he took an equally large bite from the plate on his left, batted his eyes, and rubbed the fingers of his left hand together thoughtfully.

Ethel's stomach knotted from the suspense.

"They're both very good." He worked his mouth around like he was having a difficult time swallowing.

"Would you like a glass of milk?" she asked.

He nodded. "Thanks, Ethel."

While she poured a glass of milk in the kitchen, she repeated her earlier prayer. *Lord, may the best sticky buns win. And whichever way it goes, help Joyce and me to handle it.* Then she returned to the living room.

Stan downed the glass of milk like he worked at Bill's Tires. For his final two bites, he rotated the order and ate the remaining half of the bun from the plate on his left and then, thoughtfully, rubbed the fingers of his left hand together. And, with only half of a bun to go, he employed his right hand to pick up the sticky-looking bun, popped it in his mouth and chewed. Then he slowly rubbed the fingers of his right hand for a final touch.

"This one," he bobbed a noticeably sticky finger toward the plate on his right, "wins."

"Aww." Joyce moaned while he rose from his chair.

"I have to get back to work, ladies. Feel free to invite me anytime you need a taster." Without lifting his hat, he started for the back door.

"Wash your hands," Ethel bellowed.

Stan chuckled and rerouted himself to the sink.

While he fumbled about in the other room, the girls quietly studied the paper plates.

"Thank you for your service," Betty said.

"Yes, thank you," Joyce said.

No one followed Stan to the door. They were all too aware of the positioning of the plates.

"Stan's plate will be lifted last," Ethel said.

Joyce nodded.

"Mildred, you go first," Ethel said.

Mildred scooted the crumbs off her winning plate onto the losing plate and turned it over. "Joyce."

Ethel didn't let her mind race.

"Betty, you're next," Sharon said.

"They were both delicious, girls. Next month, I think we should do a low-salt bakeoff." Betty turned over her winning plate. "One for Ethel."

Slowly, Sharon turned her plate over and stared at it wide-eyed. "Another one for Ethel."

"Two against one," Mildred said.

"There's still a chance that it's a tie," Joyce whispered.

Heads turned to eye Stan's plate.

Betty shook her head. She didn't have the heart to be in charge.

Mildred reached to her left and, with a roll of her meaty wrist, flipped over the plate. "Ethel."

Chapter Twenty-three

Ethel stared at the Scrabble board. Ireland's Sauce, with a little salt and vanilla added, had won. Not to mention the aged whipping cream.

"I'm trying to be a good loser," Joyce patted a hand above her heart, "but this is hard. Losing twice to Ethel in one season is harder than I expected it to be. She's never been a baker before . . . and now . . . ." Over the top of her glasses, Joyce eyed her through a sheen of tears, "you're one of the best."

Ethel wanted to give her a big old hug, but she couldn't because the table was in the way.

"Sharon, can you take a picture of Joyce and me in the kitchen with our sticky buns? I don't have enough pictures of me with my friend Joyce."

Joyce wiped a tear.

In the kitchen, they held up plates of sticky buns while Sharon took pictures—one for Joyce and one for Ethel to put on her fridge.

They returned to the game table, and Joyce dabbed at her eyes.

As soon as Ethel sat down, she remembered the prize. "I'm sorry to ask, Joyce, did you remember to bring the recipe for your dinner rolls?"

Joyce nodded and without a peep, reached into her apron pocket and passed the recipe cards around the table like they were playing Pinochle.

Her neighbor had surprised her, being such a good sport, and even sharing her family's secret recipe with all of the girls.

Joyce's Famous Dinner Rolls was written across the top of the 4x6 card. For years, Ethel had been after this recipe, and it was finally hers. The ingredient list didn't appear all that exciting: Flour, yeast, salt, sugar . . . But recipes could fool you.

Ethel slid the card into her apron pocket for safe keeping.

"I've never eaten two sticky buns in one sitting before in my life. And bean dip to boot," Betty sighed.

"Oh, that reminds me." Leaning over, Mildred picked up her purse off the floor. And after a few seconds of digging around, she produced the bottle of Beano.

Hallelujah! Ethel hadn't had to be obvious and ask for it.

"Oh, shoot! There's only one left." Mildred frowned. "Sorry, girls." She popped the pill into her mouth and chased it down with the rest of her coffee.

Oh, no, what now? Ethel peered around the table at her dear, sweet, elderly friends. What had she done?

"The sticky buns were *so* good," Sharon said. "Probably a hundred thousand calories apiece, but how often do we get to be judges for a baking contest?"

"I have a wonderful Fruit Cake that I serve at Christmas time," Joyce said.

"That's nice." There was no way Ethel was baking ever again.

"The Christmas Fruitcake Contest!" Sharon cried.

"Whose turn is it?" Mildred asked, studying the board.

"I can't wait. I've always loved fruitcake." Sharon's shoulders wiggled.

"How can anyone even talk about food? I'm so full," Betty groaned.

In about two hours, when the side effects hit from the bean dip and her soured whipping cream—one week past the shelf date and left open for five days in the fridge—a Christmas fruitcake contest would be the last thing on these girls' minds.

Too bad Mildred had been out of Beano.

The End.

The Sticky Buns Challenge
– is also available in Audio
Narrated by Valerie Gilbert
Audible.com

Sign up for new releases at Sherri's website
www.christianromances.com
The next story in the Ethel King Series:
Sticky Spelling
The working title for Book 3 - coming in 2018
– God willing.

Acknowledgements

A heartfelt thank you to my three main editors: Patty Slack, my line editor/story editor. You weren't afraid to be tough on me - and did a fantastic job; Kristi Weber, my final editor, thank you for meeting a tough deadline and rewriting my wrongs. And, my family editors: my daughter, Cori Murray, my mother, Ethel Schoenborn; and my godmother, Pam Waddell. Thank you!

A big thank you to Steve Janke from the Latah County Fairgrounds, for fielding my numerous questions regarding awards, ribbons, buildings . . . Thank you, Steve!

To my husband, Dave, and our son, Casey, for being my taste testers and putting up with my mishaps in the kitchen. And, for their blatant honesty which inspired many of Harold's and Jimmy's comments.

The soured whipping cream was an actual event that happened in my kitchen and inspired much of this book. Sadly, the side-effects are real! My apologies to my family.

To my mom's game girls, for participating in the mini-Sticky Bun Contest. That was a fun, fattening day! Elaine, Kristi, Karel, Brenda, Roberta, Peg . . . and of course, my mom, Ethel.

To fellow Christian writer Traci Hilton (cozy mysteries) who inspired the title of "Sticky Buns" during our critique group night.

To writing coach, Randy Ingermanson, and our critique group—Lydia, John, Patty, Jill, Traci, Jean and Mary Grace—for your help and encouragement.

Photo credit: Alison Meyer Photography for the picture of the Palouse on the cover.

The Sticky Bun winning recipe is from *Taste of Home*. On my website www.christianromances.com, I have a link to this winning recipe. Their copyright did not allow me to post it in paperback.

I've also included another sticky bun sauce recipe on page 203 that my taste-testers enjoyed.

Other Romances by Sherri

Sticky Notes Series:
Sticky Notes – Book One
The Sticky Buns Challenge – Book Two

Counterfeit Princess Series:
The Piano Girl – for ages 10 to 107
The Viola Girl – for ages 10 to 107

Standalone Romances:
Fried Chicken and Gravy
A Wife and a River

Ethel's Sticky Bun Sauce

This is a variation to try and the sauce that won Ethel the contest. This is the appropriate amount of sauce for a 9 x 13-inch pan. Use half this sauce for an 8-inch square pan.

Don't add any whipping cream for this variation.

1 cup butter (2 sticks)
1 ½ cups packed brown sugar
½ teaspoon salt
1 teaspoon vanilla
Pinch cinnamon (optional)
And of course – toasted pecans whole or roughly chopped.

Directions:

Melt the butter in the pan over medium-low heat. Add the remaining ingredients. Stir well and pour into the bottom of your 9 x 13-inch pan.

I was going to put in one of my favorite meatloaf recipes, but when I made it recently for the book, it didn't turn out so wonderful. So, I will need to revise it before submitting. If you were hoping for a meatloaf recipe to be included, please email me or join my newsletter. I often post recipes that I'm working on or have recently discovered in my newsletter. My apologies in the meantime.

God bless you,
Sherri

Email: christianromances@gmail.com
Website: www.christianromances.com

72656606R00116

Made in the USA
Columbia, SC
25 June 2017